ROTATION
PLAN

Housewife Down

Housewife Down

Alison Penton Harper

W F HOWES LTD

This large print edition published in 2006 by
W F Howes Ltd
Unit 4, Rearsby Business Park, Gaddesby Lane,
Rearsby, Leicester LE7 4YH

1 3 5 7 9 10 8 6 4 2

First published in the United Kingdom in 2005
by Pan Books

A CIP catalogue record for this book is available
from the British Library

ISBN 1 84632 407 6

Typeset by Palimpsest Book Production Limited,
Polmont, Stirlingshire
Printed and bound in Great Britain
by Antony Rowe Ltd, Chippenham, Wilts.

To Mum and Dad
(who've only tried to kill each other once)

For busy housewives everywhere,
Whose minds may wander, here and there.

CONTENTS

CHAPTER 1

AGONY

I don't remember when I shelved the dreams I had wished for myself as a girl. I don't remember when it all stopped mattering. All those years before, they had seemed so important, so un-negotiable. All these years later, they are distant childhood memories.

I used to tune into Anna Raeburn's lunchtime agony phone-in on Talk Radio many moons ago. It made for fascinating listening. All those people with car-crash lives. It's easy to feel magnanimous from the safety of your kitchen table while a sorry tale unfolds from some poor woman trying to traverse her way through a clearly ghastly marriage to a wastrel of a husband.

This particular charmer evidently preferred the horses to his family responsibilities and had converted the spare bedroom into a sort of do-it-yourself virtual bookies', having commandeered the children's homework computer and rigged it up to every online betting shop on the internet. She could tell he was gambling heavily at the moment because he was always shouting at everyone and sweating excessively. Incredibly, she

1

wasn't calling about the gambling habit. She was ringing in to bemoan his removal of the family PC because no one could get to it any more and the kids were driving her round the bend.

I recall that at the time I was making fresh pasta and secretly adoring every moment of the lengthy ritual. The fine feel of the dry wheatflour running through my fingers. The cool block of marble on which I would tenderly cajole the pale yellow dough. The long ribbons of fresh pasta falling from the miniature mangle. The peaceful feeling I hold inside.

Then there was the daily company of *Woman's Hour* on Radio Four. I would listen closely to the presenter extolling the virtues of a superwoman who had climbed mountains and helped refugees in parts of the world I had never even heard of, and another who sailed the oceans taking her husband and children with her, shaping their home-spun education despite the most spartan of living arrangements in far-flung places.

I tried to imagine the beauty of these lands and the adventure of it all.

I've never had children. This was not a conscious decision, it is just the way things have worked out. I suppose there is still time if I'm quick about it, but I doubt I ever will. Instead I labour for hours and give birth to complicated menus, nurturing each dish with a mother's love, raising my pastry to perfection.

★　　★　　★

One such day, I sat at the kitchen table shelling the fresh peas I had made a special trip to the greengrocer to buy that morning. It was time for the agony phone-in, and I was sitting comfortably. Before long, a woman burst onto the airwaves complaining bitterly about the state of her marriage. Her husband treated her like a domestic slave, brutally ignored her vain attempts at conversation, never lifted a finger to help, nor brought her flowers, nor shared a word of kindness. The list went on and on. And so did she. The catalyst for the call was that today he had forgotten her birthday.

'How long have you been married?' Anna asked.

'Thirty-two years.'

'And you expect him to change?!'

I realized that I had stopped shelling and was just sitting there, stock-still, staring out of the window. My comfort zone had completely disappeared.

My God, I thought. That's me.

I suppose now that I had misinterpreted my life of suburban comfort for happiness. The respectable full-length curtains. The newly appointed steel cooker with the superfluous extra gas ring. The neatly manicured garden. Sufficient housekeeping to shop freely at Sainsbury's but not quite enough to stretch to Waitrose. All this and more had lulled me into a moribund state which I had somehow mistaken for fulfilment. It wasn't quite what I'd had in mind when I married Robert fifteen years ago. All those promises wrapped up in a heavenly white dress and a cripplingly expensive reception filled with people I barely knew.

The agonized caller was me.

The circumstances slightly different perhaps, but the situation just the same and her pointless loveless marriage my own. Not in the dinner-thrown-at-the-wall-because-it's-too-salty sense, but in the diminution of my entire self over a long, long time to make way for a boor. It had been a stealthy, gradual erosion, a not-so-gentle brainwashing. Now I saw that mine had been washed whiter than the beautiful sheets billowing dutifully on the line in the gentle breeze outside.

The cracks had begun with the small, withering remarks as his sparkling career failed to materialize. Stuck on the middle rung of mediocrity, he had supplemented his dented ego and crumbling self-esteem by whittling away at mine. I must have been clever as a child. I had passed my eleven-plus with flying colours and had gone to the very best of grammar schools. Great potential, they'd said. Well look at me now.

I used to feel invincible, and thought that I had arrived as my husband's equal, yet the constant chip-chipping away, scathing remarks and daily cricisms eventually took their toll. I was reduced to a husk of my former effervescent self and began to take solace in the daily routine of my drudgery. My friends had gradually dropped away, finally tiring of the brittle veneer that had to be maintained in my husband's company, which had to be endured if they wanted to see me. The occasional stolen lunch dates had become so difficult to keep in the face of a querulous husband, who was determined that I should not have any interests outside of his needs, that I had simply stopped going. So the friends stopped asking, and I hid myself away among the well-organized jars and tins on the pantry shelves.

What had started as love gave way to simpering tolerance, then silent resentment, and finally a weary acceptance of my lot. Fear of the unknown and a misplaced sense of loyalty had somehow precluded me from ever seriously considering the consequences of divorce. This was what marriage was like. It was ultimately about endurance, not love. Robert was happy enough now. He had everything pretty much sewn up.

And here was I, gratefully clinging to the wreckage.

I sat there and looked at the peas. Hundreds of them, all the same, and somehow it felt significant. For the first time in many years I wondered what on earth I was doing.

I resisted the urge to throw the bowl into the bin. I have nothing against peas. Besides, there was a pretentious dinner to prepare for my husband's closest colleagues tonight, and while I was feeling rebellious in that instant, I had insufficient courage to write a triumphant Dear John letter and leave it on the dining-room table in lieu of the meal.

I brooded over those peas for a long while, contemplating my sad and meaningless existence, and wondering what had happened to the bright young thing who had once lived on red wine and pâté and pleased herself. Perhaps if I stared at the peas for long enough they would yield an answer, but they just stared back and said nothing.

I put them in the fridge alongside the ridiculously complicated marinade I had spent the entirety of yesterday afternoon constructing while listening to the man whose wife had refused him sex for the past eight years.

'Get a new wife,' Anna had prescribed. I found myself thinking what I might do if Anna said to me, 'Get a new husband,' and defiantly reached down for the bottle of white wine strictly reserved for poaching fish. I heard Anna saying to me, 'Pour yourself a glass of wine and go take a long hot bath.'

Who was I to argue? The woman obviously knew her onions.

The sound of the car on the drive woke me with a start. A panic-stricken glance at the clock confirmed the hideous inevitability that I had indeed fallen asleep. By my reckoning I had about twenty seconds to compose myself and look normal. It was a tall order. No clothes, no hair, no face, in a manner of speaking. I threw on a robe and quickly scrolled four rollers into my sleep-mangled fringe.

As I pinned the last of them into place, I suddenly remembered the beef. By now, it was supposed to have been four hours into a slow braise with the incredible marinade, not festering on the worktop where I had left it at lunchtime. Too late now. As I reached the landing, I found myself recounting all the thoughts that had danced through my head earlier that afternoon and felt deep, red anger that beef carbonnade should matter in my life. It didn't, and nor would I let it. No more.

The front door opened.

'Helen?' called the husband.

I was not yet ready to speak. I wished I could disappear into the ether right then, that very second, and never return to see the fallout.

'Helen!' This time much louder as car keys hit the console table in the hall.

From the top of the stairs I could see him. I watched him walk into the kitchen, open the fridge and then close it, open the oven and then close it.

'He-len!'

Now he was yelling.

'Hello, darling.' I had swept silently down the stairs and attempted to waft nonchalantly into the kitchen.

'Where's the dinner?' he said crossly, looking visibly anxious, but I was ready for him and bravely tried to wave away his concern with a gesture of my hand.

'Oh it's one of those cook-it-all-at-the-last-minute recipes. You know, hours of preparation and all that. How was your day?' I remembered to smile.

'You're cutting it a bit fine, aren't you? And just look at the state of you!'

'Everything's under control,' I said reassuringly.

I realized this needed to be convincing so, as a finishing authentic touch, I went in for a welcome home kiss on the cheek. Big mistake. His eyes widened in alarm.

'Have you been *drinking*?' The accusation was hurled hard, and he reeled away from me to allow me to take in the full extent of his horror. 'What the hell do you think you're doing?'

My nerve was starting to unravel.

'Oh nonsense, darling! It was just a glass of wine while I was preparing the dinner.' I made a mental note to extricate myself as quickly as possible to dispose of the empty bottle I must have left in the bathroom.

'You know how important this is. Christ,' he said, lifting his hand to his forehead as though faced with a presidential crisis. 'I bet Graham doesn't have to deal with shit like this from Sheila.'

'Well, lucky old Graham,' I muttered.

'What?'

'Oh nothing.' Now just wasn't the time. 'Why don't you go and take a nice shower and I'll get the dinner on. In fact, I'll pop upstairs and get it running for you.' I was already on my way back up the stairs to remove the evidence of my treacherous afternoon.

Back in the kitchen, things were pretty serious. So was my head. I remembered from my freedom years that the trick is to keep drinking once you've started at lunchtime, otherwise a five o'clock hangover kicks in and you're pretty much done for. Dinner was already hanging in tatters and it was only half past six. Right. Improvise. Quick. Think Ainsley Harriott, twenty minutes, and get on with it. And that was how braising beef ended up thinly disguised as filet mignon, the marinade an eye-wateringly strong sauce, and the peas – well, peas is peas.

The husband reappeared, calmer, cleaner and dressed in his usual light-blue shirt and slacks ensemble. God, did I really marry that? I should ask for my money back.

'That looks interesting,' he said, peering at the raw steaks.

It'll taste bloody interesting too, I thought mutinously.

'I'm just nipping upstairs to sort my hair out.'

'Well hurry up about it. They'll be here in half an hour. Did you open the wine? Where is it?'

I stopped in my tracks. Would that be the wine that I was supposed to pick up from the wine merchants this afternoon? I supposed it would have to be. I turned to face the music.

'I'm so sorry, darling,' I said meekly. 'I completely forgot about the wine.'

'You did what?'

Oh here we go.

'What the hell do you mean, you forgot the wine?'

He wasn't waiting for an answer.

'That's just typical. How can you forget something so very simple when you have absolutely nothing to do all day except ponce around and watch daytime TV? Aren't you capable of anything?' I assumed it was another rhetorical question. 'Well you'll just have to go and get it now, won't you?' He turned away, paint-stripping over.

'I can't.' This was not going to go down well. 'I've had a glass of wine.'

'Of course you bloody well can.'

'All right then. Two glasses. Big ones,' I added defiantly.

The look said it all. As did the brusque shove past me and the animated snatching of the keys from the table. As did the huffing strides towards the car, and the skidding wheels and the unnecessarily *Miami Vice* tyre marks left on the drive.

The evening's freeloaders arrived. Drinks were drunk. Seats were taken. The starter was uneventful, seasoned as it was with stultifying conversation about sales legends and golf shots that got away. Then came the steak. I watched surreptitiously as the first mouthfuls were consumed, my husband being the last to raise his fork. I watched him intently. He chewed. And chewed. And his eyes slowly widened and then fixed upon me a dart of sheer horror before lapsing into dazed confusion as he looked back at the steak. I was, after all, the most envied of cooks. I smiled sweetly and returned my gaze to my own plate. As if sensing the moment of tension (or perhaps tasting it) Graham the sycophant decided to reopen the conversation with his usual blinding eloquence.

'So how's that car of yours going, Rob?'

'Great. Apart from the moron who nearly ran me off the road today. Honestly, some people should be shot,' responded my husband as the others nodded understandingly.

'Again?' I asked.

He stopped eating and glared at me. I didn't usually join in much of the conversation at these things, except to small-talk with the other long-suffering wives. And after the earlier run-in, I think he was expecting the rest of the evening to pass without having to engage with me at all.

'Pardon?'

I looked up and decided to run with it. 'Well, only yesterday you were saying about how someone nearly ran into the back of you at a roundabout. And then there was that incident on Sunday when you were coming home on the motorway,' I said quietly.

'What's that supposed to mean?' He was

attempting to keep things light, but managing only to sound rather churlish.

'Nothing. It's just that you do seem to have an awful lot of things happen to you in the car.'

'No I don't!' He enforced the point, angrily digging the spikes of his fork into a cowering Jersey Royal.

'Well you certainly have a lot more than me.' I knew I probably should have stopped talking at that point, but I was starting to enjoy myself. 'I don't have people nearly running me off the road on a daily basis or cutting me up or driving into the back of me like you do.'

'That's because you drive like a hesitant snail.'

Appreciative laughter from the executives.

'I'm not slow. I'm safe.' My tone was surprisingly even. 'And I don't see the point of always trying to get ahead of the car in front, nor do I believe that the entire road belongs exclusively to me.'

'Nor do I.'

'Yes you do!' The situation was now getting nicely out of hand for a business dinner. 'What about the poor chap whose bicycle mudguard got caught up in your bumper when you refused to give him room?'

'His fault.' Husband was now adopting a school-yard folded-arm pose.

'Rubbish! I was there!' I was feeling braver now and soldiered on with 'In fact I think you are the worst driver I have ever seen.'

Judging by the icy silence, this may have been

a bridge too far. To call your husband a terrible driver in front of a table-load of guests is tantamount to taking out a full-page advertisement in every national newspaper saying that he has a microscopic penis and likes to dress up in women's clothes at the weekends. You see them occasionally in shopping centres and big supermarkets. They're the ones who dress like the Queen with sensible shoes and a matching handbag, but nothing appears to be even slightly worn. A scarf tied jauntily around the Adam's apple is a dead giveaway, as are jelly-mould wigs and shovel-like hands. Didn't you ever wonder who buys the strappy size elevens you see in the outsize 'ladies' shoe departments? Well, now you know.

'I think someone's had too much wine,' he said to the table. Ah yes, when all else fails, roll out a condescending old chestnut and pronounce the wife drunk or insane.

'And I think that you couldn't pass a driving test now if your life depended on it,' I retorted.

The morons guffawed in unison at the ridiculous challenge, and my husband joined in the braying laughter.

'I'm serious,' I said levelly. 'You pass a driving test and I'll eat my hat.'

'It would be preferable to eating this.' He went for the culinary jugular, noisily discarding his cutlery on his plate in protest.

'Unless of course you don't want to because you think you'd fail,' I chided.

'Don't be ridiculous.'

By now he was well and truly down the great dead-end alleyway of male pride, and the boss's wife didn't even attempt to mask her delight at this full-on domestic spat at the dining table. She dabbed at her lips with her napkin before smiling broadly and announcing, 'Well would you believe it? My brother-in-law is a driving examiner! He lives just around the corner. Oh Robert, you absolutely must.' Full of wine, and thoroughly enjoying the opportunity to stir things up even more, she continued, 'I'm sure he'd be only too happy to oblige!' She laughed. 'That is, of course, unless you think Helen's right?' Her eyes fixed on my husband.

And so the die was cast.

The brother-in-law's name was Andrew. He arrived looking like Catweazle the following Saturday morning behind the wheel of a maroon Skoda. The sign on the roof announced Drive Right with a test-passing slogan emblazoned across the doors.

'I'm not getting in that,' sulked the husband.

'That's all right!' enthused Catweazle as he bounded towards us. 'We can take yours!'

So in they got, and off they went, pulling away in an exaggerated manner after much checking of mirrors and conspicuous signalling. Graham and Sheila had come along to watch the entertainment and we waved them off from the end of the drive.

'Fancy a coffee?' I said.

'Definitely,' said Graham. 'And I expect you've got some of your legendary almond cakes at the ready.'

The action moved into the kitchen.

Meanwhite, a car drove around the suburbs, still checking mirrors and signalling wildly, reversing around corners and insisting on finding the steepest incline for the obligatory hill start. He could afford the bravado. It was an automatic.

'So you're doing this to stop the old woman nagging, are you?' Andy laughed. 'I heard about the dinner party. Sounds like a riot!'

'You bet,' came the venomous reply. 'And when I get back I'll be making a few changes. If she thinks she's got one over on me, she's got another think coming. Bloody vindictive bitch. She's been like a millstone around my neck for years. Now we'll see who's laughing. I can't wait to see her face when I tell her.'

'Tell her what?' asked Andy.

'Give it a couple of days. You'll hear.'

Their concentration turned away from the conspiratorial revelations and back to the task at hand.

'We'll do the emergency stop in a minute,' chipped in Andy. 'You know the drill. I whop my paper on the dashboard and you bring the car to a controlled halt.'

'You mean stand on the anchors,' confirmed Robert knowledgeably.

A few hundred yards further down leafy Acacia Grove, Andy suddenly hit the dashboard. In one huge and violent move, Robert slammed hard on the brake, forcing it to the floor. There was a sickening screech and an almighty bang as the airbags exploded into the car. Smoke poured in from the dashboard, Then everything went black.

I guess it must have been two hours later before Graham became concerned. I had tried Robert's mobile once but it rang back at us from the hall table where it had been left.

'Must have gone to the pub,' offered Graham. 'I think we'll go and join them. Sheila?' Oh please do, I prayed, my face aching from the fixed smile I had adopted in response to her incessant wittering.

It was almost four o'clock when the doorbell rang.

No keys, I thought to myself as I went to answer it. I opened the door, and there standing in front of me were the police in the form of a middle-aged WPC with a sturdy girth and a young constable with a nasty-looking spot on his right cheek.

'Mrs Robbins?' offered the WPC.

'Yes?' This is rather unusual, I thought.

'I'm WPC Wingrove from the community police team and this is my colleague, Constable Grey. May we come in?' She was soft and friendly in her manner.

They looked sympathetic and they wanted to come in. This probably wasn't about the next-door-neighbour's cat systematically picking off the other neighbour's racing pigeons.

'Has something happened?' I asked stupidly. I don't know what I was feeling at this point, except that the police turning up on one's doorstep on a Saturday afternoon looking sympathetic and wanting to come in is not normally a good sign.

'Well, if we could just step in for a minute.' She looked like she was going to anyway, so I stood aside and motioned them in while attempting to get my increasingly wild imagination in check. She turned to face me as I closed the door.

'I'm afraid we have some bad news about your husband, Mrs Robbins,' she said.

I felt my face flush red, veins pounding. My mind was racing and I couldn't speak. A hot, white whooshing noise filled my ears. Something had happened to my husband and it was bad enough to warrant a visit from the police. Not a phone call from the hospital, but a visit, in person, from two police officers.

He's dead, I thought to myself.

This was the scenario that I had so often entertained during those evil fantasies that I inadvertently indulged myself in during the twilight minutes just as I drifted off to sleep at night, and now it had come true. All those times when he was late coming home from work, imagining that some terrible fate had befallen him and playing the scene

17

over and over in my head with different plots, scripting my response, feeling the sympathy and attention. Picturing what I would wear to the funeral and how people would comfort me as I stood there bravely, shouldering the enormous burden of my grief. Dreaming how I would rebuild my life and how it would feel to start over.

But then the car would arrive, every time.

Now here I was, standing in the hallway with two police officers, and I knew what was coming. He's dead and everyone would know I did it because I wished it so. My mind raced on. Oh my God, he's not dead. He's horribly maimed but mentally intact and now I'm going to have to nurse him for the rest of my miserable days while he tortures me with his cruel dependency and I'll never be able to leave him because everyone will think that I'm evil and despicable and the guilt will eat me alive. Oh my God. It's worse. He's sustained serious head injuries and been left with the mental capacity of a small child, and he's incontinent and I'm going to have to deal with . . .

'Mrs Robbins?' I had drifted far, far away and the WPC was looking at me quizzically, her hand gently touching my arm to bring me back.

'Mrs Robbins, I really think we should sit down.' Then, turning to Constable Cheek Spot, 'Gary, go and see if you can find a kettle and a tea bag in the kitchen, would you?'

She led me through the open door of the sitting

room and we sat together on the same sofa. She began.

'There was an accident this afternoon involving your husband's car.' Her voice was quiet and concerned, and she waited for me to understand before moving on, very slowly. 'An ambulance was on the scene within minutes, and both your husband and his passenger were taken to the Royal Infirmary. The trauma team did everything possible to revive him, but he never regained consciousness. I'm afraid your husband passed away an hour ago, Mrs Robbins. I am most desperately sorry.'

My mouth was open. My eyes wide and staring. Everything moved into slow motion. It's true. He's dead. I felt as though I should say something, but instead my mouth stayed wide and my head moved from side to side, as though asking a million questions through the abominable silence.

'There were no other vehicles involved,' she continued, her hand on my arm in a non-invasive way, just as she was shown in the community policing iworkshop. 'Your husband's passenger is expected to make a full recovery so we should be able to find out exactly what happened. It seems that the airbags went off spontaneously and we're not ruling out a fault on the car.'

But I wasn't hearing any of it. No words, just muffled sounds. My thoughts were in an airlock. *He's dead. It's the only thing I know but I don't believe it. He's dead and I'm free.*

'Is there someone you would like us to call for

you? Someone who can come and stay with you for a couple of days?' The WPC was speaking in the softest tones and the young constable had appeared with the tea.

After a long moment, I heard my voice from a distant room, 'My sister.'

I was staring numbly at the wedding photograph on the mantelpiece, and my gaze passed silently through the smiling couple and began to drown in the swirling memories of a life beyond the fairy-tale picture, the life before all dreams were forgotten. In the corner of the photograph, I can just see the sleeve of my sister's bridesmaid's dress. She had hated it of course.

The WPC had the telephone in her hand, and was softly voicing, 'What's the number?'

'I don't know,' I replied. 'We haven't spoken for thirteen years.'

CHAPTER 2

SISTERHOOD

'It's okay,' Julia said, 'everything's going to be all right.'

Julia's entrance had been swift and sure. She was upon me immediately I answered the door, whispering tender words of comfort into my ear as she gathered me into her arms. The years of distance between us fell away, and I felt as though my heart would break. It was late. The distantly familiar smell of her perfume filled my senses and I suddenly felt terribly tired and unmanageably emotional. The feeling of being held like that once more by my big sister was almost too much to bear. In that moment, I felt like a child again. Safe, warm, loved and secure.

'David's here too.' Julia released me and I saw David clearly silhouetted in the doorway behind her, not knowing quite where to look, or quite what to say.

'Hello, David,' I attempted, but it came out hidden somewhere deep within a hideously muffled sob. The smile I had tried so hard to ready for him crumpled on my trembling lips and I could feel the prickling sensation of the tears that welled up uncontrollably in my poor, swollen eyes.

'Oh, Helen.' David stepped towards me immediately, wrapping his generous frame around my shaking shoulders and rocking me gently from side to side. 'We've missed you so much.' His head rested on top of mine and he stroked my hair softly and held me close. Julia watched for a moment then turned away to busy herself with the bags David had dropped by the door before she too lost her composure.

As the small, strange reunion began to settle, WPC Wingrove appeared in the doorway of the sitting room, regulation handbag slung over her shoulder and behatted into her official role once again.

She had become 'Jane' over the past six hours. A reliable, open and honest person who gave of herself freely to offer me a solid, immediate friendship under the most tragic of circumstances. We were just two ordinary women, and I wondered how often she had to do this kind of thing. You know, turning up on a stranger's doorstep in the middle of an ordinary day to tell them that their husband is dead. It can't be easy. Jane had dispatched the young and rather uncomfortable-looking constable back to the station some hours ago before settling herself in for the duration until the cavalry arrived.

I lost count of the number of cups of tea we drank, and after the serious business of official duties had been taken care of, Jane had done her level best to keep me company and to find regular conversation beyond the omnipresent shadow of a sudden death. It must have taken some great effort on her part, as I had spent most of the time staring into space, unable to concentrate on anything. Each time Jane attempted to kick off a conversation to hurry the dragging minutes along, I found that I had completely forgotten what she had said the moment she finished the sentence, so it had all become a bit one-sided.

We talked about places that we had been to on holiday. She told me enthusiastically about her walking break in the Lake District that spring, and of the one she was planning to take in Austria later in the year. I hadn't meant to appear rude, but I have always felt that anyone who plans their hard-earned leisure time around hiking and pot-holing through the Cairngorms must have something seriously wrong with them, and I was unable to muster much interest. I got the impression that she didn't share her life with a man, and nor was she the kind of woman who would want to, if you see what I mean. Good for you, I thought.

Now, hours later, Jane finally looked both satisfied and relieved that her ward was well catered for, and made ready to leave the scene.

'I'll be in touch, Helen,' she said as she stepped

out of the door. 'And if there is anything you need, well, you've got the number.'

Julia was already in the kitchen busying herself with finding the tea-making paraphernalia, but had managed only to come up with a kettle and one tea bag, and had no idea where the cups were. I stayed where I was for a little while and watched her. My beautiful sister. Tall, strong, elegant. Great in a shipwreck.

As David and I reached the kitchen we all stopped where we were and looked at each other. It was one of those moments I shall always remember, frozen in time, when no one needs to say anything, because there is absolutely nothing that can be said. In that instant there was just a quiet calm as we resigned ourselves to the extra- ordinary nature of the day.

'David's not staying.' Julia broke the silence.

'I'm afraid not,' he smiled apologetically. 'I've got a work commitment early in the morning and, well, I just wanted to come and give you a hug. We all love you, you know.' Then, passionately, 'Shit, Helen. I can't believe we weren't here for you.' The distress on his face was so unfair. We had all suffered enough under the regime of my husband's marriage. It was over now. No more tears.

'You are now,' I said.

David finished his tea quickly and gave Julia a kiss on the cheek. 'Gotta go,' he said to her.

'Thanks for coming. It was wonderful to see

you,' I said. 'I really appreciate it.' He was a good man to hug. Big, strong, generous, and gentle through and through.

And with that, Julia and I were alone.

We stood there together and looked into each other's eyes. It had been a long, long time. Too long. And at that moment, we both saw and felt the pain of the loss we had suffered, the brutality of our separation hanging there in the air above the kitchen table. All those years, advertising themselves on the visibly older faces and colour-restored hair, lost forever, never to be recovered. How could I have let such a thing happen?

Soon after the wedding, things had perceptibly altered in my newly-wed life. It had been a difficult time for us both, a big period of adjustment, but there was no denying that Robert had become downright rude. I had been told by married friends that the first year is the hardest. Perhaps it's the delayed reaction to the commitment, realizing that you've gone and painted your sitting room with a colour that you actually don't like at all. You have to learn to live with it. Or stop using the sitting room. Or change the colour, although the prospect of that is just too much aggravation.

I thought Robert had something on his mind. That this too would pass. That things would get better. And while I waited for the improvement that never came, I adjusted as much as I could to accommodate the new set of rules although they seemed to change each time I started to get the hang of them.

That particular day, or more specifically, the last day that I saw Julia and David, we had been invited to Sunday lunch at their house. I was dreading it. The journey in the car deteriorated into the usual hurling of indiscriminate insults to passing motorists, interspersed with vitriolic criticism of everything and anything about our imminent hosts.

'So. Sunday lunch again with the ball-breaker and her obedient boyfriend. God, he's a tosser, with his poofy designer clothes, and she's a consumer victim with her considerably-richer-than-thou industrial coffee machine.'

I had learned that the best way to handle these interminable journeys was to ignore him, so I would try to concentrate on the scenery and occupy my mind with other thoughts. An Indian man on Radio Four earlier that week had talked most convincingly about the virtues of daily meditation. It had sounded to me like the answer to just about everything, but I couldn't do it. Try as I might to clear my mind and think of running water and lotus blossoms, my brain simply refused to de-clutter and my lotus blossoms would invariably morph into a shopping list or sponge recipe.

Mile after mile, the torrent had continued, until I could stand it no longer.

'Oh for God's sake, Robert.' I could feel my blood pressure rising. 'She's not like that at all and you know it. You're acting like the jealous brother-in-law and it makes you look completely stupid. You just can't handle it that some women are successful in their own right.' I stared out of the passenger side window not wanting to look at his face.

'Successful? Pah! We all know how women like that make their money. I don't care how you dress it up.'

'That's enough.' My heart was sinking fast. Not again. I really thought that today I had it cracked and we would manage to get from a to b without lapsing into another *Groundhog Day* argument. This time I turned to look at him.

'Why do you always insist on doing this? I mean, just what is the point of coming here if you're going to turn it into a massive argument every time? I could have come on my own, but no, you have to come too and make it unpleasant. Why do you have to be so bloody aggressive?'

He started laughing then. His mean, nasty laugh. The one that said, 'Oh shut up, you stupid woman.' And I knew that he'd done it again, and I'd taken the bait, and so he'd got exactly what he wanted.

The fact was that Robert had always detested my sister. With hindsight, I don't think he liked any woman much at all, unless she was either tied to a kitchen sink or hero-worshipping the nearest man. Thinking about it now, I guess that he couldn't have liked me much either. There is little that is worse than feeling like a fool.

☆   ☆   ☆

I'm not sure how many G&Ts he got through before lunch, only that it was at least two too many. He had been largely silent except to snort at the newly finished extension which really was quite magnificent and blended in seamlessly with the original charms of the lovely house.

'You paid how much?' he sneered at Julia. 'God. You could tell they were dealing with a woman!' Guffaw, guffaw.

As Julia and I cleared the table after a difficult and petulant lunch, Julia suddenly put down the plates she was carrying, paused for a moment, then turned to face me, her hands resting behind her, holding on to the side of the Belfast sink. As she started to talk, I understood why she felt in need of the support.

'Look, Helen, we both know that you've made a terrible mistake,' she said. 'You look drawn and tired, you're quiet, we hardly hear from you any more. You barely even speak to your friends.' She was gathering pace, the words tumbling from her mouth. 'You have no idea how much I know. I've had Leoni on the phone. My God, you two have been friends forever and she now says she can't get hold of you at all! She's left messages but you don't call her back. And she's not the only one. I'm starting to feel like your own personal missing person bureau. You've got to do something about it, Helen,' she pleaded. 'Everyone's out of their minds with worry.'

As I stood there and tried to think of a plausible

response, the missile came flying in from the doorway and exploded in the room with a deafening 'Get your coat, we're leaving!'

Robert's face was puce as he lurched at us from the doorway. Julia and I froze.

'Now!' he screamed.

I fled past him into the hall. As I ran towards the cloakroom, loud angry shouts filled the air.

'You fucking interfering bitch.'

Robert was always pretty nasty when he was angry. Being drunk to boot just added a new dimension.

'Don't even try it, Robert.' Julia was dead calm in her response, but I could hear in her voice that she was deeply shaken. 'You don't even come close to scaring me. I know what you're doing to my sister and if you think I'm going to stand by and watch you're very much mistaken.'

I was already heading out onto the drive. David was looking up at the house from the front lawn when he saw me running blindly towards the car. He dropped the hammer he was holding and ran towards the heated voices now steaming through the kitchen window. I stood by the car and watched. The noise level increased for a moment as David's cry of 'What the hell?' joined the shouting voices, then suddenly it stopped.

Moments later, Robert emerged angrily through the front door, hand clutching at his nose but not quite managing to obscure the glaring red patch rapidly spreading across his face. He was striding towards me, gesticulating furiously with his other hand, pointing at me, and shouting, 'Get in the car! Just get in the car and drive!'

The letter arrived a couple of days later, identifiable by the orchestral handwriting on the crisp white envelope. Julia had written:

> *Darling Helen,*
> *We cannot bear to see what is happening to you, and we certainly can't stand by and watch Robert's appalling behaviour any more. I don't understand why you have not left him, but I do understand that this is none of my business.*
>
> *Maybe I've misinterpreted the whole situation, but I don't think so and Sunday was the icing on the cake. David is still very upset and I didn't think I would ever see the day that he felt compelled to hit a man. You are my sister and what hurts you hurts me.*
>
> *I know you will understand why we will never speak to Robert or have him in our home again, but you will always be welcome. I also want you to know that there will always be a safe and loving place for you here if you need somewhere to go. I love you.*

She had signed it 'Skin' and had enclosed a freshly cut key.

★   ★   ★

And that was pretty much that. The row between Robert and me blew over eventually, but the price was high. Far higher than the cost of the new kitchen that Robert indulged me with during the ensuing period of guilt. Anyway, it was easier now that Julia and David were out of the picture, and I kidded myself that my loyalties should lie with my husband, and that if I gave up this one last thing, I would be able to make a success of my pitiful marriage. The fact is, I was scared. Soon, there would be no one at all who could spot the facade. No one who could possibly know the secrets that dwelt deep within my heart. And I carefully closed down and mothballed another part of me and put it in the attic with the others.

'I adore you, you know,' said Julia, and we hugged each other with a long-overdue hold that felt like home.

'You too,' I said.

Oddly, we didn't talk much that evening. The being together was enough. We just sat with each other, exchanging affection here and there, passing the box of tissues, laughing at inappropriate moments, dissolving into tears again. The fatigue finally got the better of me and I acquiesced to the weight of my eyes.

'Come on.' Julia led me out of the kitchen towards the stairs.

'Things will seem different in the morning.'

CHAPTER 3

AWAKENINGS

I must have slept for the longest imaginable time. A deep, merciful, dream-filled sleep, full of people and places, feelings and sounds. The music of birdsong seeped into my fantasy, and when my eyes opened I must still have been drifting somewhere in that beautiful dreamland. I felt as though I was floating on a cloud, high above my house and the street where I lived, way up above all the cars and the people, carried along endlessly by angels under their expansive, protective wings.

In my mind's eye I could see the sun, already high in the sky, through the small chink in the cream linen-look curtains which I had hung so carefully not two months before. They didn't look like linen at all I observed critically, but I had convinced myself that no one knows what linen really looks like and that Laurence Llewelyn-Bowen had come to my house personally and congratulated me on my excellent choice. Examining them now, it had to be said that they were a bit rubbish actually, with a fake unfinished appearance which just looked like an enormous fault running through the entire length of the fabric, and now I felt embarrassed by their presence. Must remember to burn them. Soon.

'Good morning.' Julia's soft voice greeted me. She looked up from the book she was reading as she sat quietly on the little white stool in front of the dressing table. I have no idea how long she had been there, watching over me like a guardian, waiting for me to wake in my own time. She stood up slowly and stretched a long, lingering, aching stretch, pulling her shoulders back and letting out a small but well-earned sigh as she put the book down.

'I'll bring us up a nice pot of tea, shall I?' and she left the room quietly.

I lay back in the silence and looked at the picture on the wall beside the dressing table. A framed print of a cottage with roses and wisteria growing around a white-painted front door, all pinned neatly into place on an abundant trellis of unlikely proportions. All the flowers in the garden were in full bloom regardless of their seasonality. Armfuls of blues and pinks and purples with hollyhocks bursting through a sea of poppies and delphiniums, trees laden with fruit, and a black and white cat curled up neatly on the doorstep. A vision of Utopia. As reported by *Country Life*.

I wondered who the artist was. Whether it was a man or a woman. Whether the cottage was real or just a figment of their imagination. Whether they had painted it out of love or duty. I'd bought it in B&Q because it went with the overall bedroom colour scheme, although 'scheme' is perhaps too grand a word for it. My design confidence was stretched badly enough when faced with one pastel swatch next to another. I thought I had done well to break free from Magnolia, although even Laurence would have had a job telling the difference between it and the Harvest Beige I had daringly settled upon for the hallway. Still, it was a start, and at least I had kept myself out of trouble by attending to the unnecessary details of my neatly emulsioned enclosure.

As my reverie came to an end and my mind finished dusting away the last whispers of my morning trance, it all suddenly came flooding back. The terrible events of the day before. The visit from the police. A short but surreal trip to the mortuary before Julia arrived, which I had blanked out. The bizarre and seemingly irrelevant questions hidden within the endless red tape and miles of shabby grey public-service corridors. The barely tolerant looks on the faces of the overworked, inconvenienced staff who did their best to maintain the conveyor belt of grief that passed through their lives day in, day out, with a suitable degree of reverence while all the time staggering under the pressure of their Government paperwork targets.

I recalled how I had felt nothing, as though it wasn't really me, and I wasn't really there. Instead I found myself walking and living the rest of yesterday in a vast, empty, vacuous void, except for the constant nagging notion somewhere in the back of my mind that this must surely be a dream: perhaps I'm still asleep? It seemed now as though I had been led on a wildly exhilarating waltz, pulled ungraciously from my gilded chair by strong, handsomely uniformed hands, and swept along reluctantly to the rousing strings of Strauss, whirled unceremoniously round and around for hours, then thrown, exhausted, back into my seat, barely able to catch my breath.

Julia appeared with a tea tray, all set out perfectly, with an egg-cup filled with daisies nestling on a saucer alongside a silver egg-spoon and a tiny pile of salt. It was a little 'cheer-you-up' joke of course. An egg, but not an egg. Much nicer. Much prettier. And who wants an egg anyway? There was a little rack of triangular toast with the crusts cut off, marmalade in another egg-cup with another little spoon, some butter, a pot of tea with all the trimmings, and it was all just perfect. A perfect breakfast tray. Exactly as I would wish for if I were first up on death row.

The panic rose in me as sharply and un-expectedly as the car that slammed into that poor pedestrian I heard about on the local news last week. God. I bet he didn't see that one coming. It wasn't even his usual route home. His stricken mother had given a heartfelt soundbite to the reporter explaining how her son really ought not to have been there, and that he never came home that way. I wondered what had made him change his mind. Did he have a premonition that he had an appointment with the Grim Reaper? Did it arrive in the form of a fancy to change direction, just once, just for that day?

The feeling that welled up inside me now was huge and cruel and crucifying. My mind was on fire, and I considered whether I shouldn't just throw myself off the roof and be done with it. That wasn't really an option. The roof's not high enough and I'd be bound to land on the neighbour's pigeon house, killing their prize flappers and ending up in court being sued for malicious damage.

Julia set the tray down.

'What am I going to do?' I asked her desperately. A ridiculous question, I know, but my eyes were pleading and, at that moment, I was truly lost.

'I don't know what to do, Julia! The funeral! The arrangements! The people! Oh my God, what's going to happen?' I hid my face in my hands and closed my eyes. Oh please. Please. Just make it all go away. I could feel my soul ebbing into the distance as surely as the tide leaves the shore.

Julia poured the tea and looked at me. Square, reliable, firm.

'It's all sorted,' she said. 'David's got Sara on to everything this morning. She's my PA. And she's unbelievable. An Exocet. But don't tell her that.

Ever.' She winked at me. She was perched on the bed by my side, buttering a piece of toast and regarding me with caution.

'But,' I protested, 'what about all the people who have to be called, and—'

'Done . . . -ish.' Julia handed me a piece of toast then took a delicate bite from one herself. 'You fell asleep pretty quickly last night, you know. You must have been exhausted. I spoke to David when he got home and he's been fantastic.'

I nodded my unsurprised response. David was always fantastic.

'It's you we need to concentrate on. You've been through enough. Let someone else take care of it.' A small pause as she put her toast down. She never has more than two bites of anything. Fascinating, really.

'How are you feeling?' Her manner was relaxed, but her question earnest and her heart anxious. I could tell. She was very good at hiding her emotions, but when you've grown up together, sharing a bedroom and fighting over whose turn it is to have the hot-water bottle on a freezing February night, you get to know someone very well indeed. She used to tell me that there was a monster living in the wardrobe behind my bed, and that it only came out at night time, and that if you put your feet down during the night when it is dark, the monster will grab your legs and drag you back in with it. It used to scare the living daylights out of me.

How am I feeling? I thought about the question and realized that I wasn't used to thinking about my feelings at all really.

Just then, the doorbell rang.

Julia stood up and announced, 'Excellent. That'll be Sara.'

Before I could ask, she was off. I followed her, as always, lagging a couple of steps behind. She swung the front door open and in leaped the vibrant Sara, dressed from head to toe in all the things that you never manage to get to the shops in time to nab for yourself. How does someone do that? The conversation between the two of them was swift and efficient, then all eyes turned to me.

'Sara's going to take care of everything and we're going out.'

'What?' I said.

'Come on. Let's get you out of this prison so you can clear your head a bit. Sara's going to answer and return any calls. She's already been on to Robert's office this morning to explain what's happened.'

'But it's Sunday!' I said.

'Sunday, Schmunday,' Sara said matter of factly and bit into a big green apple from the fruit bowl on the hall table. 'They're alive, they've got a phone, I'll find 'em.' Her eyes narrowed to a squint. Must have been a sharp one. She was staring into the apple, munching as she spoke, unfazed by the sanctity of the Sabbath.

The thing about Sara, you see, is that she's one

of those girls you don't mess with. She wants to speak to you? You're going to speak to her and that's all there is to it. She's from Lancashire, kickboxes to keep fit, plays the piano like a demon, and loves her job because she gets her bonuses paid in shoes. Good ones. Like the Manolos you see in *Vogue*. Tax free.

'Sara will tell everyone that you've gone away for a few days with your sister to get your head together,' Julia said. I didn't reply. Just stood there gawping, yet again, as though it was becoming my speciality. 'Helen, listen to me. It's all under control.'

As I stood there in my dressing gown in front of these two women, I wondered how come I had never delivered someone a fait accompli like that. A sentence that really said what it meant, and really meant what it said. No ifs. No buts. And I wondered how come some women end up like them, and other ones end up like me? What makes us different? Is it laziness? Is it fear? *Are* we different? Oh stop it. It's all too complicated.

Suddenly Sara was upon me, looking deep into my eyes as if to hypnotize me into concentration, still eating the apple, and saying to me, in the authoritative tones you only get from a sage twenty-two-year-old, that I was not to worry for a single moment, and that everything would be taken care of, and that if anyone needed to contact me she would call me on my mobile. She's got a law degree, you know.

I haven't got a mobile, I thought.

'And here's your mobile.' She put a little shiny black object into my hand.

Hello, I thought to myself, that looks rather minty. I turned it over and looked at it. Nokia, it said. Now I know that this sounds completely ridiculous, but suddenly I felt just a little more important than I'd felt a few moments before. Do I have a mobile? Why yes! Of course I do, silly! I imagined the embarrassingly stupid question from the fictitious person who had popped into my head while I practised having a mobile. I tried not to admire it as I noticed Sara crawling around the sitting-room floor searching for all the phone sockets that Julia had unplugged the night before as she'd moved around the house, silencing the potential intrusions before they happened, shutting out the world with every curtain she closed. I looked at Julia. She was smiling at me her special half smile that loved me so well. I appreciated it.

'Come on,' she said and nodded me back towards the bedroom. 'Let's get you dressed and get the hell out of here.'

We reached the bedroom and she went in ahead of me. She straightened the duvet, threw open the curtains, turned and flung open the closet doors.

A few hesitant seconds passed. This time it was Julia's mouth that opened in horror with a stunned, gaping silence. Her eyes widened as she took in the reeling nightmare before her and mutely surveyed the hideous contents of my sadly neglected wardrobe. I admit, I had lost my way somewhere along the line from a fashion point of view.

'Jesus Henry Christ,' she said slowly as she lifted out a short yellow jacket with white buttons crammed onto a hanger with two equally offensive tops. She held the garment away from her face as though dealing with something nasty she had found blocking the plughole and peered back into the wardrobe.

'What *have* you been wearing?' she asked incredulously as she continued to pull things out of the closet and throw them onto the bed, her face staging a chorus line of expressions as each new disaster revealed itself. 'And what the hell's *this*?'

'It's a gypsy top.' I sighed. 'And no, I'm not proud of it.'

'Gypsy top? You mean maternity smock.' And she dropped it onto the floor. 'God, Helen, since when did you start wearing florals? I can't believe the stuff you've got in here. Look at this one!'

Now, the particular blouse currently wilting under Julia's scornful radar I had to admit was a pretty peculiar decision. A pastel assault of abstract geraniums in Neapolitan colours rising to a theatrical Jane Eyre crescendo with its lace-trimmed leg-of-mutton sleeves. It was truly a triumph in bad taste. Why I hadn't thrown it away I don't know. I guess that I had thought that having a full wardrobe was better than having an empty one, regardless of the embarrassing rubbish inside.

Julia was now getting into her stride, hauling

things out of the closet indiscriminately, dumping most of them onto piles on the floor and setting other pieces aside on the bed. I didn't mind. I had thrown in the towel with them all long ago, and each time I had determined to tackle the task of purging my clothes, I managed only to make a terrible mess and give myself an awful headache. It was about time someone took the matter in hand and did something about my outer pack-aging, and I was relieved that the task had fallen to my sister rather than finding myself on the receiving end of the fashion Gestapo at the front door in the form of a BBC camera crew flanked by the insufferably bossy Skinny and Susannah.

'Oooh, those are nice!' Julia tossed a pair of sage-green trousers at me. 'Stick those on.' I had worn them only once. They fitted really nicely around the bottom and made my legs look longer but Robert had said that they didn't suit me. As I pulled them on now, I remembered how much I liked them. I zipped them up and looked at their reflection in the mirror inside the wardrobe door, turning sideways so that I could see my rear view. Could be a lot worse, I thought. I put on the plain white shirt that Julia had left on the bed.

'I'm just going to have a word with Sara,' she said. 'You take your time and get ready. Pop a bit of lipstick on, brighten your face up a bit. That'll make you feel better.' And with that she made her way downstairs.

I sat at the dressing table and looked at my face

in the mirror. It looked the same to me as it always had. Older, yes, but essentially the same. I think it must be something to do with the eyes.

When you look deep into someone's eyes and remove judgement from your heart, you really can see them properly. Now, staring intensely into my own, I knew it was the same old me, secreted somewhere inside, but having been kept in solitary confinement for so long that perhaps it would never want to come out again. Like taking a captive animal back to its native environment and insisting on setting it free after years of conditioning. The door opens at the end of a long uncomfortable journey and the animal just sits there ungratefully, refusing to budge until the gamekeeper pokes it with a big stick, forcing it to leave the protection of the cage and rejoin the vast wonderland that is Mother Nature. The conservationists feel elated and deeply moved by the goodness of their act. Of course, the moment the cameras are dismantled and the humans have returned home from their feel-good field trip, the poor animal is taken down by the haunches and eaten alive by the first predator it meets.

The doors of my cage had been opened. I reached for my make-up bag and made ready to face my own reserve.

'That's better!' appraised Julia as she walked back into the room trailing a handful of black bin liners behind her and dumping them onto the bed.

'Thanks,' I said. I didn't usually bother with make-up, and the fifteen minutes in front of the mirror had indeed created something of a transformation. Not in a curtain-back, before-and-after, TV-moment way, but enough to disguise the tears that I had shed as I tried to brush the painful memories out of my hair. I shifted on the seat and turned towards her.

'So where are we going?' I asked. Julia helped herself to my hairbrush and set about her crowning glory with vigour. She put down the brush and smoothed her hair with her hands before answering.

'Selfridges!' she beamed.

CHAPTER 4

SHOE FETISH, ANYONE?

Julia once told me that she wants to have her ashes scattered in Selfridges' shoe department. It's one of the few places where she feels truly happy and fulfilled, and she has been known to spend so long in there that one of the assistants once had to go and bring her some lunch. Her reputation now precedes her, and seeing as most of the staff are on commission, Julia's arrival can cause something of a stampede.

'Just ignore anyone who tries to pounce on us,' she whispered to me as we walked in. 'We only get served by Tony today, okay?'

'Why?'

'You'll see.'

'Joooo-leee-aaaah!' oozed the lady in the Chanel concession. 'You looking for something special today? We have the new collections in and I know you will simply love—' Julia cut her off.

'Is Tony around?'

The lady's warm smile chilled off noticeably as the prize customer was lost to the charms of the young man who had already spotted us from the far corner of the floor. He waved at Julia and ushered a couple of customers out of his way, both of whom had obviously thought for a moment that they were at last in danger of getting some service.

'Darling!' he said, and kissed Julia's cheeks. 'And who is this?'

He was already looking me up and down. Please, don't look at my shoes. I hadn't thought about them until now, but all of a sudden I would rather have been bare-footed than standing there in my sensible— Oh God, I can't say it, I can't say it . . . they're from Marks & Sparks.

'My sister, Helen.'

'Aahhhh!' he said, as though everything now became clear.

'We want to try on some shoes, Tony. You choose.'

Getting a man to pick out shoes for us to try on? You cannot be serious. I looked at Julia and furrowed my brow in a what-on-earth-do-you-think-you're-doing expression.

'I have exactly the thing,' he announced confidently. 'You just wait until you see them. They will make you go completely insane.'

He raised his hand to his fevered brow and disappeared off to the stock room. Julia smiled at me.

'This,' she said, 'is one of the all-time top experiences to have before you die.'

She wasn't wrong.

Tony came back holding several boxes containing shoes so exquisite and delicate that they might well have been crafted by Cupid. But, according to

Julia, it wasn't the shoes we were after. I sat in one of the more spacious and comfortable chairs and waited to see what would happen. Tony knelt down in front of me, reached out and took hold of my ankle, cupping it gently in his right hand. His left hand then slid gracefully up to my calf, and he slipped off the shoe that I was wearing. Both hands lingered for a moment before he removed one to reach for the first pair.

The hairs stood up on the back of my neck and I felt my face flush scarlet.

I shot Julia a look of such alarm that she had to turn away quickly before she burst out laughing. Tony then proceeded to caress my feet into a selection of styles, delicately fastening the teeny little straps and buckles, letting his fingers rest on my skin here and there, supporting my lower leg even when it didn't need it, and softly massaging the arch when he removed each one and lowered my foot gently to the carpet.

He was completely transfixed. I was absolutely speechless. I swear I have never had such an erotic experience (regardless of whether or not it was in public) in my entire life. How I managed not to start moaning and rolling my head around I don't know. I've never been a smoker, but, my God, did I need a post-coital cigarette. And I'm sure my hair wasn't that curly when I sat down.

'Get ze red. Eez fabulous!'

Simoné had the strangest accent I had ever

heard. A sort of mix between broad mid-European (whatever that was) with a bit of South American thrown in. He was small and perfectly formed, rather like the naughty artiste once again known as Prince. Pocket-sized maybe, but every lady should have one. He was gazing knowledgeably at the dress, head slightly cocked to one side, stepping backwards with his hands clasped together at his chest in reverent prayer at the altar of Ghost.

'Eez fabulous, yes?' he repeated, nodding constantly at Julia who nodded back without a hint of a smile.

'Yes,' she said. 'I rather think it is. You have to get it in the red as well,' Julia confirmed to me. 'Simoné, bag it and tag it and put it with the others.' She flashed me a smile, widening her eyes in conspiratorial fashion, before whispering to me the holy grail she had so dedicated her life to.

'Personal shoppers!' she breathed. 'A godsend,' and broke into a broad grin.

Simoné was flapping huge sheets of tissue paper around, waving his arms at his underling, a poor mousy-looking girl who looked far too frightened to try to hold together an air of stylishness in a designer concession. How on earth did she end up working here? Surely she'd be more comfortable knocking up lunchtime bagels in a sandwich shop or something?

Things were not going well for Simoné.

'Beeger bags! Get me some beeger bags now!'

he wailed, glancing at us and explaining, 'Theez is not going to work!'

He flailed his arms around and shook his head in submission as the perfectly adequate carrier bag failed to live up to his tissue-holding expectations, and he threw it to the floor in disgust.

'I sorry,' he apologized. 'No one here know anything. I ask, but I don't get anything. Eez useless. Eez totally ridiculous. I cannot believe.' He shook his head and did that Gallic gesture of shrugging with huge animation, eyes rolling madly. 'You theenk that they would know. But they don't. Eez amazing really. Amaaazing.' He looked over his shoulder, and shrilled rather louder than he had intended, 'Ze bags!' Then, looking back at us, 'My God in the absolute heaven madly,' he said bizarrely, absently tidying his already perfect hair in a moment of acute stress.

We were now all standing around waiting for the bags. Simoné was smiling uncomfortably and trying not to fiddle with the pens. He sighed and looked away, then removed an invisible thread from the glass counter top. An almost imperceptible shift in Julia's stance indicated clearly enough that this pause was rapidly upgrading to an unacceptable delay.

'You like my top?' Simoné asked conversationally, opening his jacket slightly and looking down at the very fine fishnet T-shirt in midnight-blue with fuchsia ribbon detail at the hip.

'Fabulous,' said Julia flatly, not even looking.

Simoné was beginning to panic so directed the rest of the conversation at me. Leaning towards me conspiratorially, closing his eyes and nodding slowly, he revealed, 'Eez for a woman!'

He regarded me as though he had just disclosed the whereabouts of the last gold seam in Wales.

'Yes! Yes!' Simoné was now nodding furiously with a beaming smile, holding the jacket wide open to give us the full, bedazzling effect. He looked around then turned back to me triumphantly, singing out loudly, 'Eez not for man! But I think, yeah! Wow! So whaat eez for woman! I think eez great! No? Yes? You think too also?'

This person is clearly unhinged, is what I thought.

'Definitely,' I said, and nodded my total, un-reserved approval.

He looked relieved, as though the gun had been temporarily removed from his temple.

The bags arrived with the flustered mouse and Simoné was so pleased to see them that he almost lost it. Then the final amount was rung into the till, and I do believe that I actually did become hysterical when I saw the total, although I managed to hide it well behind my tiny whimper of 'That much?'

As we moved away from Simoné's delicious theatre of dreams, I couldn't help but express my concern to Julia. This was no longer fun, and I felt completely and utterly out of my depth.

'Julia, we have to stop now, I just can't afford

all this. I really think that's enough.' But she was already two strides ahead of me, forcing me to quicken my pace to her side.

'Is the credit card still working?' she clipped.

'Well yes, but . . .'

'But nothing. If the card works, we shop. When the card stops working, we stop shopping. Right?' She was still walking, still focused, and by the looks of it, definitely still shopping.

'But I'm only supposed to use it for emergencies,' I explained meekly.

Julia stopped, dropped her head a little and let out an exasperated sigh before looking at me and saying, 'And what, precisely, do you call this?'

Deciding to take a break, Julia and I had taken up temporary residence in one of the cafes on the second floor. Très chic, I thought, and wondered if ignoring the customers was also considered fashionable in a modern-fusion sort of way. Finally, someone appeared at our table to take our order.

'Two glasses of champagne and two cappuccinos, please.'

'Julia!' I protested too much, pretending to be horrified at her order for fear of what the sullen-looking waitress might think of us asking for champagne at this hour. I have no idea at what point in my life I had started worrying about what complete strangers might think of me, and made a mental note to try not to apologize for my wishes, or indeed for my very existence in future.

Before I had time to file it under pending, Julia stood up and said, 'I don't believe it. There's Leoni.'

Leoni was already weaving her way towards us through the other tables. As she reached our hearing, I could clearly see the concern on her face. It had been a long time, and other than the immediate worry lines, I have to say that she was looking good.

'I hope you don't mind.' Her eyes darted between me and Julia, then back again. 'I spoke to David this morning, then Sara, and she said you'd be here. I've been wandering around the store for ages looking for you.' She stopped to catch her breath before our eyes met. 'I'm so sorry, Helen. I'm just so—' and she burst into tears.

I put my arms around her and felt her pain. The sight of the tears on her face stirred something within me. Sorrow for her, perhaps. Feeling bad that she should be feeling so awful at that moment, and realizing that it's not only the person to whom events happen who necessarily gets tangled up in the emotional wreckage.

Julia's 'How are you feeling?' question had been on my mind a lot since my waking hour, and I had found that I wasn't feeling much of anything at all. Just a bit dazed and confused. And deeply scared now and again.

Leoni and I hugged for a while, and I brushed her tears away with a smile. 'It's okay, Leoni, it's just a bit of a weird day today. For everyone.'

'I hear that,' said Julia, then she raised her voice towards the waitress who was halfway to our table with our order, busily spilling most of the coffee onto the tray as she clumsily negotiated her way through the tables and chairs. 'You had better make that a bottle, please. Three glasses. And hold the cappuccinos.'

I don't know if it was the champagne or the shopping, but it felt like one of those summer days you want to hold in your hands forever. Looking up at the sky through the branches of a tree as you lie in the park. Making daisy chains. The intoxicating smell of freshly mown grass lacing the stillness of the air. Being in love with a boy who doesn't even know you exist. Wondering if it's because you haven't got any breasts yet. Those were the days.

There were so many bags that Julia had to call Sara at my house and get her to work out the logistics. Julia had mentioned that Sara had sounded strangely out of breath when she called.

Sara hadn't bothered to explain that she had spent the past hour stumbling around in the garage where she had eventually hit upon a circular saw and welder's mask which she had then man-handled up to the study and virtually destroyed Robert's locked desk with.

Drawer then well and truly open, she had made short work of the fact-finding mission and had little difficulty in identifying the interesting transactions she found detailed in the bank statements and other papers she had uncovered. Credit card receipts, phone bills, it was all there. An envelope shoved towards the back of the drawer was marked 'insurances'.

'That was jolly well done of you,' Sara had smiled as she pulled it out.

She'd tipped out the contents of the big Manila envelope and spread them across the desk, scanning each one briefly but carefully before setting it down. She'd looked around for a piece of paper and, finding none, settled on using the back of an envelope and immediately began scribbling notes. Every now and again she would stop and rummage through the papers to check something then go back to her intensive note taking.

When she had finished, Sara turned her attention back to the drawer. It wouldn't pull all the way out, so she had to bend down and peer into the back of it then lean herself right back rather awkwardly to reach in with her hand. As her fingers tried to feel the back of the drawer, they touched upon something soft and velvety. She'd pulled it out. A little black velvet box. She'd opened it, and inside was a simple but most beautiful diamond ring. As she looked at it, she had noticed a little piece of paper stuck inside the top of the box. She'd carefully picked at the side of it with her nail, easing it down until she could get hold of it and pull it out.

That's when Sara's phone had rung from the

kitchen table. She quickly returned the note to the lid and slipped the box into her pocket before running to take the call.

It was from us, exhausted and shopped out, with too many bags by far.

Sara sent a courier van to collect the booty while Julia and I headed back to the house under our own steam. My feet ached and I felt ashamed.

'Hi, chicks!' Sara beamed as we walked in through the door. 'I can't believe you had to get a van for all your stuff! That's brilliant, that is!' and she squeezed herself past us, lighting a cigarette as she hopped out onto the step.

'Nor can I,' I said quietly, my voice now betraying my increasing concern.

'Well, I don't know what you're worried about!' Sara threw her head back and laughed as she blew a plume of smoke from her fruity-salved lips. 'I found a load of paperwork. Really, really interesting! I've bagged it all up to take round to the lawyer's office in the morning. Hope you don't mind.'

My brain was tired. My feet were killing me, literally, and I gave Sara a glance which said, 'Look, I don't know you, right? And I know you're here to help, supposedly, but now you're really starting to get on my nerves.' Sara looked back at me levelly, then at Julia, then back at me.

'You,' she said, pointing her lit cigarette towards me, 'are seriously loaded.'

Julia must have detected the look of fatigue and bemusement on my face, because she immediately started ushering Sara away.

'You really should get going,' she said to her. 'Thanks a million for all your help today and don't worry about getting in on time in the morning. I'll see you when I see you.'

'Cheers!' said Sara brightly and she went off to gather her stuff together.

'I'll walk you out to the car,' said Julia.

'Thanks, Sara,' I said, suddenly contrite. 'I just don't know what to say.' I shook my head. I really was truly grateful that she had been there that day. I could see why she was Julia's chosen one and why it had taken her two years to find just the right person to support her acrobatic life.

'Don't mention it,' Sara said breezily. Her manner and voice were soft and friendly. It was quite a contradiction to the person I had met earlier that day. Julia was already outside as Sara disappeared through the door and I turned towards the kitchen.

By the time Julia arrived to join me, her tea was almost cold. I had eaten all but one of the biscuits and now sat there looking at the shameful evidence and wishing that I had either replaced the biscuits or cleared the crumby plate away with its telltale lone occupant, hastily disposing of that one just as I had done the others, rather than putting it in the bin or trying to struggle it back into the packet.

Julia ignored the tea.

'Have you got any brandy?' she said.

'In the cabinet in the sitting room,' I told her.

She was already on her way and came back with the bottle.

'Glasses?' she said.

'Up there.' I pointed.

She nodded one towards me. 'No thanks,' I said. 'You go ahead.'

Julia helped herself to a modest measure, sat at the table and crossed her long legs.

'Sara said for me to tell you sorry about the desk,' Julia said.

'What desk?'

'Robert's desk upstairs. The lock was a bit stiff apparently.'

'Oh,' I said, not really hearing or caring. My mind was everywhere.

'And something else,' added Julia.

'What?'

'This.' She took a black velvet ring box from her coat pocket and put it on the table in front of me. I looked at it without touching it, then looked back at Julia questioningly.

'Sara found it in Robert's desk,' she said.

I looked back at the box. It's a ring box, I thought. I couldn't imagine why a ring box would be locked away in Robert's drawer. I didn't want to touch it. Why on earth was there a ring box locked away in Robert's drawer? I thought that if I opened the box, he would pop out, like a huge genie, and he would be real again. Or I would wake up and find that this was indeed just a huge, epic dream. The car would arrive safely at home, yet again. And Robert would be back.

'Well open it!' insisted Julia.

I picked it up and snapped open the top of the box. It gave out a little creak. And I gave out a little gasp. It was beautiful. A simple solitaire diamond, set into a gleaming white band.

'Holy shit,' whispered Julia. 'I think you just found your birthday present.'

I stared down at the ring. As I inspected it more closely, I noticed a little piece of paper tucked into the top of the box. It dropped out easily. It said: *I love you. Robert x.*

I passed it to Julia and took the ring out of the box. Julia read the note and looked at me. I slipped the ring onto my finger. It was just a bit too big. Still, hardly surprising given the years that it'd been since Robert gave me a piece of jewellery. It never even crossed my mind that maybe it wasn't actually intended for me.

'It doesn't fit,' I said.

CHAPTER 5

IT'S YOUR FUNERAL

Seeing Leoni again after such a long time had unsettled me somewhat. Although we had talked a great deal during our brief reunion in the cafe on Sunday, there was still so much that had been left unsaid. I guess that the test of a true friendship is to see whether you can walk through their kitchen door after more than a decade and pick up the conversation exactly where you left off. That was the way it had felt, and I was humbled that Leoni had saved my blushes over the way I had just abandoned our friendship. After paying the premiums since adolescence, it was rotten of me to run off with her investment. But I think that we were so pleased to see each other again that she would have forgiven me anything. It was an honourable gesture, and she can't have known how much it had meant to me.

Julia was only too pleased to encourage me to spend time catching up and suggested we drive over to Leoni's to spot her for a cup of coffee.

As we approached the front door, I could see that Leoni was waiting for us impatiently and looking highly concerned.

'It's Millie,' she said. 'She's got the most awful hacking cough on top of the dreadful cold she's had for the last week and I have to dash out to the chemist to pick up a prescription.' She was already heading towards her car. 'I'll be back in twenty minutes.'

'Oh no,' said Julia, and we both looked at the front door which Leoni had left ajar behind her.

'Behold, the gates of hell,' she whispered to me as we gingerly stepped over the threshold. The noise was both immediate and head-splitting.

'Cruella! It's Cruella!' screamed the twins as they appeared from behind the door. William was waving a plastic sword around dangerously and Joshua burst forth to reveal an impressive armoury of vacuum-formed guns hanging from the various belts and straps he had cunningly attached to his head and body. They were running towards the stairs when Julia caught Josh by one of his commando belts and pulled him back with a sharp jolt. William stopped on the stairs and made a load roaring noise as he flailed his sword in Julia's general direction.

Julia raised her voice sternly and silenced the twins into a lucid moment.

'Now, boys,' she said, 'we're not going to hurt each other today, are we?' and she raised a fist towards them and pulled a hideously twisted face.

The twins looked at each other, launched into another ear-piercing scream and raced off together up the stairs. Julia smiled to herself before noticing the little figure standing in the doorway of the sitting room, dressed in cosy pink pyjamas with appliqué elephants, clutching a teddy under her arm and sucking her thumb. Julia walked towards her slowly then bent down and squatted onto her haunches.

'Well, hello there, little Miss Millie.' She smiled softly at the little girl and touched the top button on her pyjamas. 'Are you feeling all rubbishy and horrid today?'

Little Miss Millie nodded her head sadly and looked at the floor.

Julia stretched her arms out and Millie reached up and held on tightly to Julia's neck. She liked it when Auntie Julia picked her up. She smelled nice and she had soft hair.

'Goodness me!' said Julia, pretending to be lifting an enormous weight, 'what on earth have you been eating?' Millie giggled and Julia laughed softly as she scooped her up into her arms and wandered through to the sitting room, settling into a comfortable armchair and gently nestling Millie in her lap.

Suddenly there was a God-almighty crash from upstairs. The light fitting shuddered and jangled and there was a loud scream of 'Oh William, you stupid idiot!' Julia flashed me a worried glance and I rushed upstairs to see what all the commotion was about. Whatever it was, it had certainly sounded pretty final. As I reached the top of the stairs, I could see that the boys' bedroom door was open and they were both standing there staring at me with wide eyes. The serious draught indicated that something structural was up, and as I reached the door I could see the smashed window in its full glory.

'It was William! It was William!' shouted Josh, pointing wildly at William's face. William slapped his brother's hand away.

'Oh shut up, Josh, you girl,' he said, his face reddening.

'William kicked the football through the window!' Josh yelled enthusiastically, shouting into my face and pointing at the window. 'He said David Beckham's a poof because he wears girls' earrings and that he can kick his head in anytime he likes and then he said watch this and then he kicked the ball really hard!'

William suddenly went for Josh and I tried to wrench them apart without causing either of them any damage. It wasn't easy, and one of the kicks meant for Josh landed agonizingly on my shin. The pain sharpened my senses and I reprioritized my tactics, grasping each one of them firmly by the ear and pulling them apart without much concern for their yelps of discomfort.

Downstairs, I found Julia still sitting in the armchair with Millie, this time with a book in her hand, softly reading to the ailing but entranced little girl with the miserable cold and the soft yellow curls. Julia played with them gently in her fingers, rolling them this way and that as she held the book wide open with her other hand so that Millie could see the pictures clearly. They were reading Millie's favourite story, *Mister Jelly*. Julia did all the characters in silly voices and every now and then she would give a little shake or shudder to give Millie the full effect. Millie would point at the page and giggle her little cartoon chipmunk laugh. It would get Julia every time, so they spent most of the story chuckling.

I looked on silently from the shadows beyond the doorway, although I knew I ought not to have done, not knowing when, or how, to enter, and I thought about a time many years ago shortly after Julia had flown the nest.

I was still at school and her sudden and unexpected departure left a big hole in our family unit which I was then expected to fill. She had come back briefly after dropping out of university. Dad was devastated. They had given up pretty much everything so that they could provide their offspring with the opportunities that they felt they never had themselves, and had put virtually all their stock in Julia who, several years my senior, had proved herself to be something of an academic superstar.

By the time I got into mainstream school, she more or less dominated all my parents' attention so I got away with coasting along and no one really taking too much notice of what I was doing. It wasn't as though I was thick or anything, just a few years too late. My mother in particular used to go to great lengths to introduce the subject of her elder daughter into her everyday conversations with neighbours and friends. It was always Julia this and Julia that. Given a couple of sherries, Mum would elevate the whole topic a couple of notches and lay out a string of accolades that Julia had yet to achieve. I think there was a big part of Mum that had failed to deliver her own expectations, so she lived those unfulfilled personal ambitions through her firstborn, striving to feel every exciting moment that Julia felt, greeting the news of each exam grade with the same elation and celebration as she would have if it were her own.

I minded a great deal at first, but then I got used to it and spent most of my time either lying around on the bed listening to my little pocket transistor radio through the ear piece or disappearing for hours on end, having decided to go and visit a friend miles away on my bike.

Now, to the collective shock of the family nation, Julia had stuck two fingers up at everyone and walked away, and suddenly it was me that was getting all the flak.

'Don't you ever go and do what your sister's done!' wailed my mother, sobbing into her tea towel.

'That's bloody gratitude for you,' added the old man, shaking his head and wondering where he went so terribly wrong. 'You give it all up, you make sacrifices, you go without everything, and for what? Me? I could have had a new car. I could have gone and joined that posh golf club up the road' (he didn't play golf), 'I could have bought myself, well, anything I wanted, but no' (big sigh), 'no, I give it all to my kids. And what do we get in return?' He gave the newspaper an enormous flap and huffed his disapproval before staring back at the crossword.

'He's right, you know,' nodded Mum, furiously drying up a tea cup then shaking her head and tuttutting before placing the cup back on the shelf with the rest of the set, perching it at exactly the same angle as the others, rosebuds facing front.

And that's how I ended up living in a soap opera, listening to the mewling, strangled cries of my fatally wounded parents, and planning my own escape. I was angry with my sister for having left such an ugly trail of devastation in her wake, with me the only Apache left. Yet in my heart I entirely understood why she had done it. It was me who had had the easy life, she who had had the daily pressure of rising to the unreasonable demands of two parents who found little comfort in each other so turned their attentions full beam onto their beloved first child.

I was something of an afterthought, and up until the point when Julia left again, I could have got away with anything, if only I had thought to do it.

'Go, Julia,' I cheered secretly in my head, and I imagined how exciting her life must now be. Free to do as she pleases. Free to be who she wants.

Free not to be what other people wanted her to be.

We would write to each other, long seductive letters filled with news and secrets, hers illustrated with funny little drawings in the margins and sometimes on the back of the envelope, and I envied her the charmed life that she seemed to be leading. That feeling went on for years and years while I watched from the sidelines and finished my own education, until, one day, Julia arrived home unexpectedly and asked if she could stay for a while.

We did think it rather odd, and her manner indicated that all was not well. Indeed, she was a lot sicker than any of us realized. It wasn't talked about, and when I saw my mother crying softly at the kitchen table when she thought no one could see her late one night, even then I had no idea of the shame she felt had been heaped upon her family. The generation above us still held some pretty strange ideas about the ways in which God moves. Especially the guilt-ridden Catholic club, of which we were all fully paid-up members.

It seemed that the good times had finally revealed their price.

For years Julia had danced and partied the nights away without the faintest idea that chlamydia was stealthily eating away at her reproductive system, and by the time she found out, it was already too late. My mother was unable to offer Julia comfort, wrapped up as she was in the certain knowledge that her golden child would now fail to deliver even the most basic of her expectations. What had she done to deserve this? Not Julia, you understand, Mum. She took ownership of her daughter's cruel fate and claimed all the pain for herself.

Julia had fallen silent for days, rarely venturing from our bedroom, scarcely eating anything at all. Despite loving her and wanting the best for her, I had always felt it so unfair that she should be the one with everything. Sometimes I had even imagined something happening to redress the balance, that she would perhaps have a grand failure in some way and that my parents would then look in my direction and notice that I too was a bright and shining star in my own way. They would realize how they had overlooked me for all those years and throw their arms open to me, begging for my forgiveness. I would be gracious of course. But please, not like this.

Now I wondered if this was my punishment, to watch my sister walk through the rest of her days with a heavy heart hidden deep within the beautiful exterior I had so envied. In her sparkling years of deliciously irresponsible behaviour she had surrendered the future gift she had never even considered. Children. The doctor was sympathetic, but she was also quite clear. There was no possibility. None at all.

Julia looked up from the armchair and caught my eye. She smiled at me and held my gaze as she lowered her head to nuzzle Millie's curls. I watched on helplessly as her expression dissolved. The unstoppable tears filled her eyes and spilled over in a generous stream, taking a little of her mascara with them, cascading silently down her cheeks, and dropping like tiny oceans onto Millie's hair.

Millie put her hand up and felt the top of her head.

'Urgh, it's all wet!' she said.

'Yes, darling,' said Julia, quickly looking away and wiping her face with the back of her hand before facing her ward. 'I was feeling sorry for silly Mister Jelly!' she said.

'That *is* silly!' said Millie, and she giggled and flung herself backwards hard into Julia's shoulders before looking up and saying, 'I love you, Auntie Julia.'

'And I love you too, pumpkin,' she said, and gave her a long hug.

We all heard the key as it slipped into the latch on the front door. In stepped Leoni, slightly out of breath, paper prescription bag in hand. She pulled her coat off and started to put down her things.

'Everything all right?' She smiled as she closed the door.

'Terrific,' said Julia. 'But you might be needing a glazier.'

'What? William! Joshua!' Leoni was already shouting as she went off in search of the culprits.

We heard her yelling, 'You wait until your father gets home!' Then some shouting from William and Joshua followed by crying and another slammed door. Leoni finished slating the boys then went in search of the Yellow Pages and sat with the telephone in the hall.

Millie had somehow managed to fall asleep amid all the rumpus and Julia set her down gently on the sofa, covering her up carefully with the woollen blanket she found lying on the arm of the chair. We crept into the kitchen and left her in peace.

Over coffee, the conversation turned to tomorrow's funeral.

'I really think you should let me come with you,' said Julia again before turning to Leoni. 'She's determined to go on her own, you know.' Julia shook her head.

'I'll be fine. Really,' I assured them. 'I'll see you at the tea.'

This was something I wanted to do alone.

I had had very little to do with the funeral arrangements thanks to the efforts of Julia's posse. There had been some initial opposition from Robert's distant family, but they soon shut up when Sara suggested they take on the responsibility of the funeral themselves. Sara had been meticulous in her approach, contacting everyone, choosing the funeral director and seeing to the formalities. Her initial plan had been to try to get away with a quick in-and-out at the county crematorium with a non-denominational service from the in-house shepherd, but this hadn't gone down particularly well with some of the family so Sara had pulled in the services of the local priest to add a certain gravitas to the proceedings. Frankly, I think Julia would have dearly loved to set fire to the corpse herself, preferably while he'd been alive.

The local reverend had insisted upon a condolence visit to the widow (that would be me) so he arrived at the allotted tea-time slot and we sat in polite awkwardness while he asked me if there were any particular lessons or hymns that I would like to include in the service. He stank of fags and booze and I suspected that he probably ought not to be driving that afternoon.

I chose a few of the old favourites, 'Abide with Me', 'The Lord Is My Shepherd', that sort of thing. Father Farrell asked me what kind of a man Robert had been and whether there were any stories about how he had affected the people around him during his lifetime. The irony wasn't lost on me. I knew what he had meant by the question – fishing about for some personal information so that during the service he could talk about Robert as though he had known him, fooling the grieving congregation into thinking he was a good man and perhaps even managing to leave a few people with the impression that he was a regular churchgoer and decent God-fearing citizen who had led a respectable, contributory life.

I could hear it now: 'Really? Well I didn't know that.'

Father Farrell couldn't possibly have known what he was really asking me. I considered his question carefully before answering this man of God.

'Robert was a good husband,' I lied.

Father Farrell nodded and smiled reassuringly. I noticed him sneaking a small, scruffy Silverline notepad and a stubby piece of pencil from his jacket pocket. His eyes never left mine, as though willing me not to notice that he needed to write this down.

'Go on,' he encouraged me.

'Well we're pretty ordinary folk really.' I shrugged, struggling to find something positive to say. 'He went to work.' I concentrated hard. 'In sales,' I added thoughtfully. 'I'm afraid I really don't know much about that.'

Father Farrell looked around the room, hoping for a prompt in a family photograph perhaps.

'Other family? Children?' he asked.

'Not that I'm aware of!' I laughed inappropriately. He made a note.

'It must have been a terrible shock for you, Mrs Robbins.'

'Yes. Yes, it was.' I nodded. 'Look, would you mind if we . . .' I stood up and smoothed down the front of my dress. 'It's just that I have so much to attend to.'

'Of course,' he said as he rose from his chair.

He put his unfinished cup of tea down on the table and picked up his hat.

'Thank you so much for coming.' I shook his hand and he nodded to me in a holy way.

'God be with you,' he said.

The crematorium was a few miles from the house, perched as it was on the edge of town where no one bothers to go unless they are either disposing of their dead or looking for a quiet spot to shag in the car. It's a grim place. A low-rise red-brick municipal building with an unforgiving square chimney stack rising high above the green tiled roof. I've never seen any smoke coming out of the chimney. I think someone once told me that they run the furnace just once a day, and that the jars of ashes they hand back to the bereaved families are literally just a few scoops of the communal remains. If they were to cremate each person separately, global warming would have caught up with us long ago.

The landscaping in the grounds is classic local council, deploying the kind of shrubs that no one would want to steal. Dark-green low-maintenance evergreens with their own natural bayonets fixed beneath the shiny leaves lest someone should decide to reach out and touch them. Plants with natural defences they call them. Who needs defending at a crematorium for heaven's sake? They're already dead. It's the live ones you have to watch out for. The public signage seems rather strange too. Commands like 'no parking' were set in sombre colours on smaller than usual placards.

I was sitting in the car alone, near to the entrance of the car park, watching other people arrive, wondering who they all were, and not knowing whether they would be attending Robert's funeral or someone else's.

Can't stay here forever, I thought, so I broke cover and wandered around to the other side of the building. Cigarette ends littered the ground like stressful confetti and I could see an earlier cloud of mourners as they emerged through the double-doors at the back. Out they filed, tissues in hand, red-eyed and all moving along doing the funeral shuffle. Like the other public services I had encountered so closely since Black Saturday, the planning was predictable and efficient, creating a path that could churn out a funeral in thirty minutes and eject the mourners through a neatly placed set of rear doors as the next bunch poured in through the front. From what I could see, there was no immediate danger of a recession in the death business.

Floral tributes were laid out in groups. One of the larger collections had a big MUM spelled out in separate letters made from yellow carnations. I wondered if she had been an old Mum or a young Mum. I decided old, otherwise the flowers would have read Mummy, and only an old person could like yellow carnations. Then again, having found out for myself how shockingly expensive funeral flowers are, perhaps the Mum decision had been a budgetary matter. I left the family of strangers to their collective grief and headed back towards the entrance.

More people had arrived while I had been hiding, and the doors to the chapel were now open again for the macabre business of dealing with the next customer. I bet they don't get many complaints here. Not much in the way of refund demands either, I expect. This time, I recognized some faces, a smattering of work colleagues, a few distant relatives whom I vaguely recalled from the wedding, several others I had met at the very rare functions Robert and I had attended over the years, his parents' own funerals included. I stood back a little, keeping my distance and not really wanting to go in or speak to anyone. The whole gathering made me think only of the years of marriage which I was now starting to bitterly resent.

The tears I had cried over the past days had all been for myself. I couldn't believe what an idiot I had been. Robert had stolen my youth, my beauty, my verve. He had taken what could have been the best years of my life, and no one here knew anything about it. Anything about me. These were Robert's people, not mine, and I didn't know if I could stand the sight of them long enough to see Robert's coffin dispatched to wherever it was he was destined for.

'Just remember,' Julia had said to me as I stood ironing my black trousers that morning, 'this is the last time you will ever have to see any of them, so just get through it and hold on to that thought.'

So I took a deep breath and braced myself as I walked into the chapel, avoiding as many eyes as I could and taking my place in the front pew which had been respectfully left empty. Father Farrell was already there, standing at the low-key pulpit, arranging his non-existent notes. He noticed my presence and nodded a smile towards me before looking up to see if his audience was now complete. It was hardly a packed house. Thirty or so people at the most. Not much to show for a lifetime of bullying.

I saw the same woman I had seen hanging around outside earlier. She would have passed my notice were it not for her frequent glances towards me. I had initially thought that she must have been with the earlier party, but now she was in here, dressed up to the nines (although I've never been a great fan of the cling-on leopard-print collar and cuff look), weeping uncontrollably. Very *Coronation Street*. Graham and Sheila seemed to know her.

I found myself wondering how many people would come to my own funeral and what Father Farrell might say about me. I closed my eyes and listened to the piped organ music playing in the background.

'Dearly beloved,' he begins. 'We are gathered here today to celebrate the life of our sister, Helen, and to pay our respects as we entrust her soul to God the Father, creator of all things, and to whom we shall all one day return.'

He looks up at the heaving congregation, a sea of weeping faces, some holding each other, some unable to stand under the weight of their grief. Father Farrell is struggling to hold on to his own emotions, pulls an enormous handkerchief from his sleeve and blows his nose noisily. The church, unable to hold the vast crowd, is filled to bursting point with mourners spilling out into the church-yard and the streets beyond, where speakers have been set up in the trees to relay the service to the masses who have travelled far and wide in response to the newspaper headlines screaming my death. Father Farrell closes his book and casts it aside.

'Those of you who knew Helen personally will forgive me if I dispense with protocol today. I have been overwhelmed by the letters and calls that I have received from so many of you, so instead of the traditional funeral service, I would like to share some of those words with you today.' And he produces a colossal box, overflowing with letters, reaches in and plucks out pages at random, reading aloud the tales told by each one sharing the gift of having known such a phenomenal woman. From somewhere outside the church, the haunted cry of a heartbroken woman calls my name to the wind before collapsing into the arms of a fellow mourner.

'Dearly beloved.' Father Farrell's voice broke through my dream, and I forced myself to open my eyes.

I looked at Robert's coffin and felt the finality of it all.

Sara had been quite right about hiring the nearest function room to contain the post-funeral refreshments rather than holding the wake at my house. She had found one to rent in the rather gloomy-looking public house on the brow of the hill just before the crematorium. We arrived to find sandwiches laid out under cling film on heavy foil platters and plastic trays readied with glasses of cheap wine. It was truly awful. I had a fleeting vision of Jilly Goulden clutching at her throat and sliding to the floor before launching into a stream of expletives in place of her usual vanilla and apricots. One sip was enough to set off a crippling piercing pain just behind the ears, as though imbibing battery acid. Perhaps best to stick to the revoltingly stewed tea.

'Helen?' Oh great. Sheila and Graham.

I stood there and listened to their sympathy as Sheila's voice began to take on the droning qualities of Charlie Brown's teacher.

'Graham and I have been trying to call you for days but I think there must be something wrong

with your phone. We understand that this is a difficult time for you and we wanted to let you know
that if there is anything you need you must call
us. All right?'

She looked at her husband for affirmation and
he nodded gravely.

'I'm going to come and see you tomorrow and
we'll see about getting your shopping and housework organized, then you'll be wanting to sort
through Robert's things, I expect, and I know that
you'll be finding everything terribly difficult so I'll
be able to stay with you for a couple of days while
you stay in bed and have a good old cry.'

'But there's really no need,' I began my futile
protest.

'Absolutely,' said Graham, helping himself to
another shot of battery acid. 'And you're not to
be shy about asking for help with all those jobs
that aren't for the little woman.' He tilted his body
towards me. 'I know what you ladies are like with
plugs and lightbulbs, and if there's anything needs
fixing around the house, I'm your man.'

Graham pointed at his chest, although I noticed
he was looking at mine, then he made to put his
arm around me. I took a step backwards and
promptly stood on someone's foot.

'I was hoping to take that honour on myself,'
came the friendly voice from behind me.

'David!' I had never been more relieved to see
a friendly face.

'Oh Graham, Sheila, may I introduce you to my

brother-in-law, David, and my sister, Julia.' They looked slightly put out.

'Oh I didn't realize you had a sister!' said Sheila, and she looked at Graham as though silly confused Helen must have made a mistake.

'She does indeed,' said Julia as she steered me away from them.

'Let's get you out of here.' Julia bent down and whispered into my ear. 'David will take care of this lot and catch us up later.' And she led me out of the Locomotion Inn towards my car.

'I'll drive,' she said, and she took the keys from my hand.

As she did, I noticed that same woman from the crematorium again. She was looking at me, but as soon as I met her gaze she turned away uncomfortably as though she had been caught staring. My pace slowed as the penny gradually dropped. I had realized long ago that Robert was probably playing away from home on the odd occasion. Men don't remove sex from their domestic agendas without putting up a fight unless they're seriously ill or getting it elsewhere. And I suppose it was more convenient for me to turn a blind eye to the odd lipstick stain than to start World War Three. It's not as though I wanted to take that particular conjugal responsibility back (heaven forbid), but I certainly hadn't banked on a full-blown mistress. Now everything fell into place, not that it mattered any more.

'Just give me a minute.' I left Julia's side and

approached the woman. She looked nervous for a moment, then defiant.

'I know who you are,' I told her, and felt nothing as I walked away.

CHAPTER 6

HOUSEWIFE DOWN

'Fucking great!' hissed Leoni as she piled herself and several large bags into the back of the limousine. Marcus was trying to hold the twins back as they screamed and cried in protest at their mother's imminent departure.

'We want to come!' wailed William, and started thumping Marcus's legs with his fists. Marcus's face was stony as he tried to pull the distressed and difficult child off his trousers while balancing the crying Millie in one arm. Leoni started to make towards them, calling instructions at Marcus about one thing and another while we watched him rapidly losing his cool.

'Leoni, just shut the bloody door and let's get going,' said Julia impatiently, and Sara reached across Leoni and pulled the door shut with a rude bang while shouting. 'Bye!'

'Okay, John! Let's move out!' Julia called through to the driver, and he pulled away in a stately fashion as we squealed like primary-school children in the back.

★   ★   ★

81

After the downer of the funeral the week before, Julia had decided that there was only one thing to do after burying one's husband, especially one like Robert. Celebrate. I can't say that I had met her suggestion with any great enthusiasm, but she and Leoni had managed to talk me into it with the promise that I wouldn't have to do a thing except be ready for collection on the Friday morning with an open mind, and some of the new clothes we had liberated from Selfridges. To be honest, it seemed to me that it was they who were desperate to get away for the weekend, not me. I had become the perfect excuse and alibi, all conveniently rolled into one.

Leoni produced a cold magnum from her outsize purple shopper. 'Go on, punk,' she said as she struggled to wrestle the wire from the cork. 'Make my fucking day.' She opened the window a couple of inches and fired the champagne stopper out into the street.

'Oi!' shouted a man as it hit a shop window, having missed his head by a whisker, but we were already gone.

'Marcus looked happy, then,' said Julia as she passed Leoni the glasses to fill.

'Bloody bastard. The twins have had an invitation to go and stay with one of their schoolfriends and my mum's offered to come over and look after Millie and cook for him.' We could all sense the steam coming from her ears as she tried to steady the enormous bottle sufficiently to fill the glasses, but with every bump and turn, they would bubble over uncontrollably, spilling onto the carpet.

She looked up to hand me a glass.

'Why is it that the one time he's supposed to have the kids he manages to farm them out to other people?' She turned her attention to Sara. 'He's got absolutely no bloody idea what it's like for me in that house.'

'You just want him to have a really hard time while you're away,' said Sara.

Leoni took an enormous swig of champagne. 'Yes I fucking well do.'

By the time we pulled up outside the grand entrance of the hotel, we were all feeling quite comfortable. Julia barked something at the doorman who immediately sprang into action and directed a couple of flunkies to deal with the bags. He turned to Julia for approval and she pressed a note into his hand before making her way to the reception desk with Sara hot on her heels. Leoni and I hung around in the foyer. I was so nervous that I felt as though I was waiting to take my driving test for the third time. That had been a nail-biting moment, especially when I realized that I had got the same examiner who failed me the first time for turning right onto a roundabout (yes, I know).

Everyone now within my viewfinder looked as if they either belonged there or probably owned the place, and I knew that they could tell just by looking at me that my natural habitat was a freshly hoovered suburban semi. I measured them all up in turn, some milling about in sharp suits being purposeful, some dressed like the secret service with little ear pieces, some deep in conversation on invisible mobile phones. I felt intimidated, so I decided to adopt an air of confidence and started looking impatiently in my handbag for my mobile. Quite what I thought I was going to do with it I don't know. Ring dial-a-disc, perhaps, and try to look exasperated in a deal-breaking kind of way.

As I pulled it out and pretended to find a number, it suddenly rang from my hand. I got such a fright that the handset almost jumped out of my grasp, forcing me to fumble like an idiot to prevent it clattering to the floor.

'Hello?' I answered nervously.

'Gotcha!' came Sara's voice, and I looked up to see her laughing at me from the check-in desk, mobile to her ear. Julia took the keys from the receptionist and motioned us towards the lift.

'We're in,' she said.

As we settled into the generously appointed suite, Sara made straight for the bathroom. 'Oh cool!' she shouted through to us. 'Molton Brown stuff!' She came back into the room holding a bathrobe and started pulling off her jacket. 'How much are the cashew nuts?' she said, making her way towards the cupboard.

'Sara judges the quality of a hotel by the price

of the nuts,' explained Julia patiently as she began taking things out of her bag.

'Yeah!' Sara chirped. 'Fourteen quid's the record so far.'

'She can also down a whole Bacardi Breezer in two and a half seconds,' added Julia without looking up from her unpacking, 'so keep her away from the minibar.'

'Two and a half seconds?' repeated Leoni. 'That's not possible.'

'Oh yes it is,' Sara announced in her best pantomime villain voice. 'Watch.'

Now this I had to see. Sara opened the little fridge and, adopting a serious expression, selected a suitable bottle. She found the bottle opener and removed the offending lid, then rummaged about busily in her handbag before pulling out a McDonald's straw still in its wrapper. She tore off the paper and held up the straw like an in-store demonstrator. 'Always carry your own equipment,' she advised strongly, and then folded the straw into a Z-shape before pushing it into the neck of the bottle.

'Ready?' she said.

Our look of eager anticipation indicated that we were.

'Right then.' And she put the bottle to her lips and threw her head back.

In one enormous evacuation, the entire contents of the bottle disappeared down Sara's throat. She didn't even appear to swallow, and she didn't spill a drop. Sara righted herself and held the bottle high above her head, upside down, then let out the most enormous belch. Her eyes were watering slightly but, apart from that, she appeared to be totally unscathed by her daredevil stunt.

'I thank you,' she said, and swept into a low curtsey.

We responded with an appreciative ripple of applause.

Something beeped loudly from Sara's handbag and she leaped across the bed to answer the alarm. She looked at the message on her Palm Pilot and snapped back into PA mode.

'Julia. Your meeting's about to arrive.'

Julia looked up from her bag.

'Bugger,' she said. 'I almost forgot about that.' She smoothed down the front of her dress, checked her appearance in the mirror and picked up her handbag. 'Listen, girls,' she explained, 'I had a meeting I couldn't cancel this afternoon so the client's coming here and I'll deal with him in reception. It shouldn't take long.' She turned to her faithful assistant.

'Sara, if I'm not back in twenty minutes come and get me. Say anything you want, but make it sound urgent. Right. Back in a bit.' And she swept out of the door.

'Okay, ladies.' Sara clapped her hands. 'Who wants to learn how to neck a bottle in two seconds, then?'

All I can say in my defence is that it seemed like

a good idea at the time. As the Government mantra goes: education, education, education.

Leoni slid open the balcony door and we stepped outside into the rising hubbub of the traffic droning reliably down Park Lane. The view across to Hyde Park brought with it memories of playing softball in the summer with friends. How we all used to arrive in the right place at the right time regardless of the fact that no one had yet even heard of text messaging, ready to spend all afternoon messing around, bringing easy things to eat and drink, never needing to get home, staying until the chill finally drove us away. I liked Leoni a lot. We went back many years and had shared a great many things together, soft-ball included. We smiled and gave each other a good long hug.

'How's Marcus?' I asked her.

Marcus, the long-suffering husband.

As we stood out there above the rising fumes, she told me about their make-or-break rough patch a few years ago.

The trouble started when her debit card was refused at the supermarket. She was so mortified that she had a go at Marcus about it and he blustered back at her saying that it was the bank's fault. But then it happened again a couple of weeks later. Marcus was being terribly difficult about it all, and then she began to get suspicious and wondered if he was having an affair and squandering their household budget on seedy hotel rooms and cheap jewellery. He was irritable and snappy with her, and she began to feel vulnerable and deeply worried.

She had determined to put it out of her mind when one day a couple of weeks later the pilot light went out on the boiler. Leoni knew roughly how to fix it but couldn't quite see what she was doing. She failed to locate the torch that was supposed to live permanently under the sink with the cleaning things, but then remembered that they always kept a spare in the glove compartment of the car. Marcus is very organized like that, but he has to make sure that it's the 'right' torch, as described in the best-gadgets features found in his just-this-side-of-porno men's glossies.

She took Marcus's car keys off the hook by the front door and made her way out to the drive. Leoni had dropped Marcus off at the station that morning as he had a business lunch to attend and didn't want to take the car, as though lunchtime drinking was compulsory to his chances of success that day. It's a tough business, insurance.

She got into the passenger side, opened the glove compartment, and was met by an avalanche of paper bursting forth under the pressure and spilling out into the footwell around her. Leoni let out a gasp as she tried to control the terrible mess before noticing the theme of the stash. She picked up a crumpled letter with the familiar bank logo that had fallen by the gearshift and read the first few lines. Her temples started to pound. She selected another at random and stared at the menacing threat from the building society, her eyes resting on the word 'unless'.

It didn't take her long to realize that she was ankle-deep in bills, statements and terrifying letters carrying big red warning messages from a whole convention of debt-collection agencies. There were dozens of envelopes, some untouched, some hastily torn open with the contents quickly scanned and then stuffed back in. The sheer volume was astounding. She forgot about the torch immediately. Instead, she now gathered up the enormous pile of thuggish correspondence and took it into the house and to the safety of her kitchen table where, piece by piece, she shakily unravelled then painfully reconstructed the devastating mountain of debt in front of her. By her reckoning, she had better prepare to say goodbye to her entire life. Elbows on the table, she rested her forlorn face in her open palms and wept bitterly.

She had sat there, numbly, all afternoon, before getting up to fetch Marcus from the station at six-thirty. It was raining. He was watching out for her and ran to the car from the shelter of the ticket office, holding his newspaper above his head as a makeshift City gent's umbrella, and got into the passenger seat beside her in his everyday way.

'Filthy weather,' he grumbled as he brushed the rain off his shoulders and head.

They journeyed the first mile or so home with

him talking about his marvellous meeting that day with the well-impressed managing director and she, as though locked in a relentless arcade game, driving through the rain-stained streets, seeing the colours of the traffic lights reflected on the wet tarmac, listening to her heart pound, trying to find sufficient courage to tell him what was waiting for him on the table at home in place of his dinner. As they pulled up at the next set of lights, she took a deep breath.

'Marcus,' she said softly. 'Are we in some kind of financial trouble?'

Well. Apparently Marcus went absolutely mental. I mean screaming-at-her-to-get-out-of-the-car mental. From the look in Leoni's eyes when she told me all this, I could tell it can't have been a good moment. He eventually finished with the ultimatum, 'If you tell anyone, I'll leave you.'

So they remortgaged the house, sold one of the cars, and moved into separate bedrooms. Some weeks later, Leoni told the Relate counsellor that she felt as though she had just taken a ten-years-backwards step.

Poor Leoni. It seemed that she had had a lot of the old electro-convulsive shock treatment over the years. She always freely and unashamedly admitted that she had married Marcus for the security, and she really did believe that she had loved him at the time. What she hadn't realized was that the Porsche was leased and the mortgage on his then Fulham address was way beyond his not-much-above-average means. But they stood united and faced the music together, and Leoni learned to dance to a different tune.

The twins had been a pretty major shock too. I have seen from a safe distance that the impact of a new baby arriving is Armageddon enough without having to face the double-whammy of a split egg. Leoni had been inconsolable during the months that followed the difficult birth. Not because of the babies, but because of the cataclysmic effect of the multiple pregnancy on her delicate size ten figure. She had blamed Marcus entirely. It was his fault that she looked like this. After trying without much success for months on end to restore herself to her former glory, she finally declared war on her body, decreed the entire area a disaster zone and imposed the fiercest sanctions. The whole community suffered, as is so often the case with these things. Marcus said that just because she looked like a big fat whale, that was no justification for having nothing to eat in the house except mung beans and rusks.

'Little do you know,' she had said slyly to herself as she did a few more tummy crunches. 'If you wanted to find cheese and chocolate you should have looked in the washing machine, shithead.'

So Marcus would stomp off to the local take-away and Leoni would eat a huge lump of Cheddar to calm her nerves. Marcus put her behaviour down to hormones and believed that he was a New Man because he emptied the kitchen bin regularly without being nagged into it. Which prompted Leoni to place viciously sharp objects just beneath the vegetable peelings in the hope he would one day cut himself horribly, so that she could watch him suffer just a little of the pain that she was now going through on a daily basis.

The boys were a real handful, and as the years passed by Leoni felt her energy being sapped as she changed from a witty, cosmopolitan girl about town into a shackled, screaming harridan. She had once gone to their family doctor and begged him to put the twins on Ritalin, even if only for the summer holidays, but he had looked at her disapprovingly and she had made friends with Prozac instead. So she upped her wine intake, increased her magazine subscriptions and had an industrial-sized lock put onto the boys' bedroom door. On those occasions when she had had enough, she would sweep into action without mercy, enforcing her own special pin-down routine, then retreat to the safety of her boudoir and disappear into long, meaningful telephone conversations with her girl-friends, or the telesales people, or anyone at all for that matter. The Jehovahs now gave that particular front door a very wide berth. They never did come back for the pamphlets.

Leoni said she managed to keep just this side of sane over the years by drinking lots of wine and having people over to dinner whenever she could convince them that the boys wouldn't vandalize their cars on the driveway again. And that yes, they would probably send them to stay with Granny on that night so no, guests wouldn't be begged to play Teenage Mutant Whorehouse Auto on the PlayStation all night.

It was during one such dinner party that they realized the other houseguest they were entertaining that week, the school rat, had escaped from its cage and was now frying horribly after one of its incisors hit a live wire as it chewed its way inside the cavity wall. Apart from the almighty smell, Bismarck the rat caused a small but devastating fire and several thousand pounds' worth of damage. They had to have the whole of the upstairs rewired. Marcus was not amused.

I suppose it was because the lights were out and there was no form of media distraction or electronic entertainment that night that Marcus somehow managed to penetrate Leoni's normally impregnable fortress later that evening. Shock number whatever, little Millie was born nine months later.

'At last,' Leoni groaned as the registrar battled to repair her impossibly war-torn labia, 'another woman in the house.'

As I settled myself into the comfortable, magazine-modern chrome and leather chair in the hotel bar, I was glad to have settled on the red dress that

Julia and Simoné talked me into, but the shoes were proving a little hazardous. My practice sessions in the bedroom seemed to have been scuppered by the velvet pile carpet, which had given me scant preparation for the skating-rink qualities of a highly polished limestone floor. I found myself sort of gingerly creeping along, as though trying to get to a bus stop in one piece on a ferociously icy morning. Sara had watched me moving around like that for a little while before she took me aside and discreetly tipped me off in a girl-friendly manner that I looked like a very badly trained French Resistance spy.

'What can I bring you, ladies?' The exquisitely lithe waitress bore a friendly expression which announced openly that she didn't see anyone on this particular table who could be considered any kind of threat to her infinitely superior good looks.

'The martini menu, please,' said Julia.

'It's there on the table,' said the waitress, tapping the top of her pen on the martini menu sitting in the middle of the table with a 'God, you must be really thick if you haven't seen it right there in front of you' tone.

'No,' said Julia coolly, 'I mean, mix it and bring it. The martini menu. All of it.'

The waitress was now confused, so Julia broke the task down into simple modules, just as she did for her less intelligent junior staff like Vicky, the stunningly pretty but unbelievably dim-witted airhead on reception.

Julia continued patiently, 'We are going to start at the top of the menu, and work our way down, until we get to the bottom of the menu. So that means you bring us one of everything. Yes?'

Now the waitress understood, and instead of writing down our order, she smacked her pen onto her pad, tucked both away in the top of her shamelessly low-waisted trousers, picked up the martini menu from the table, and gave us a big, broad smile.

'Coming right up.' And she walked over to the bar to relay the order. The three bar staff gradually stopped what they were doing and gathered around as she leaned over to quietly announce the unexpected sporting fixture seated in the bar. They all looked across at our table, then one of them gave us the international okay sign with his thumb and forefinger.

I don't remember terribly much else about the next couple of hours.

'Get another lychee one,' slurred Sara as she squinted into the bottom of the empty martini glass. 'This one's horrible.'

'I think I'm going to be sick,' said Leoni.

'No you're not,' said Julia. 'Just remember to breathe and you'll be fine.'

Leoni tried to straighten herself up and took some exaggeratedly deep breaths.

'Not like that, Leoni. You'll pass out.' I rubbed her arm and felt deeply relieved that I'd managed to avoid some of the drinking by mixing up the glasses when no one was looking. The fruity ones had been awfully moreish, but I had felt the effects of the third one before I was even halfway through it and had decided that the shoes would almost certainly kill me if I let another drop pass my lips.

'Let's go out clubbing!' Sara demanded in a flash of inspiration. 'Where shall we go?'

'Well I don't know anywhere, I'm afraid,' I offered uselessly.

'What about that place down the King's Road?' shouted Leoni unnecessarily loudly.

'God, Leoni, that was in the Jurassic period,' said Sara, trying to scrape the last remnants out of the empty raspberry martini glass. 'It's really crap now, full of sad old estate agents who call themselves property developers.' She did that double-finger inverted-comma gesture and then tried to lick the inside of the glass.

Julia let out an exasperated sigh and banged her hand on the table. 'Don't give me problems. Give me solutions. Now get back to me.' She got up from the table and headed towards the ladies' room, her lofty gait ever so slightly punctuated by the tiniest wobble in her step.

By the time Julia got back to the table, Sara, Leoni and I had gathered ourselves and Leoni's breathing had returned to normal.

'Are you feeling a little better now?' I asked her. She hiccupped, gave me an unsteady thumbs-up and tried to wink a big affirmative.

'Great,' she said enthusiastically as she tried to force her eyelids to open properly.

'Right,' said Julia, 'here's the plan.'

And we synchronized our watches and headed over the top.

Outside in the open air it was a beautiful evening in the city. Warm and fuelled by diesel, filled with light pollution, and brimming with the excitement of young people embarking on the infinite possibilities of a still youthful Friday night. The noise of the traffic was soft and calming after the throb of the music in the bar, so we decided to walk and talk for a while, peering into windows as we strolled along and pointing out which flats and houses we would like to have if we won the lottery. As we walked around the crescent of a beautiful garden square, I saw the one for me. An elegant, white stucco-fronted house with bay trees at each side of the shiny black-lacquered front door and gleaming brass fittings. That would do very nicely, I thought to myself. Then I noticed Julia looking around anxiously with a pained expression on her face.

'Julia? Are you all right?' I went to her side and touched her arm.

'I'm absolutely busting for a wee,' she said urgently, crossing her legs and bobbing up and down like a parrot on a stand. Now, those who know Julia also know that her waterworks are notorious. Something to do with the gynaecological problems she had earlier in life. Her weak bladder usually behaves itself but, once she starts drinking, all bets are off. Sara knew the score, and immediately started looking around for the nearest sign of convenience. Nothing. Not a pub, restaurant or public loo in sight. Julia was starting to panic, then said, 'Oh sod it,' and nipped through the gate of the exquisite townhouse I had stood in front of and imagined was mine. She made a quick dash for the large terracotta pot centred on the pebbled patio masterpiece, pulling up her coat and skirt as she squatted down behind it.

'Keep a lookout!' she hissed at us, so we milled about a little and tried to make ourselves look inconspicuous as the sound of running water and Julia's huge sigh of relief settled onto the heavy evening air.

The floodlights came on like something out of *The Great Escape*, showering the front of the house in a thousand megawatts of bright white light, quickly followed by a crescendo of polite, elderly laughter as the gleaming black front door opened to reveal a formally dressed dinner party of eight alighting onto the spotless steps. Julia might as well have been peeing centre stage at the London Palladium.

'Great Scott!' boomed the man with the monacle as it dropped from his eye. And at that moment, more than any other in my entire life, I just wished I had a camera. The women gasped, hands flying to their mouths. The men stared and tried to conceal their stupefied faces by waffling expressions of 'Well I've never seen anything like it' and things like that while poor Julia tried in vain to stop the River Kwai as it rolled several martinis' worth of torrent towards the pathway they were about to step onto.

Julia looked up towards them. 'Good evening,' she said apologetically. 'I'm most dreadfully sorry.'

Quickly recovering from the interruption to her evening's impromptu performance, she reluctantly put the damp tissue into her pocket and pulled her clothing back into place. She steadied herself against the side of the enormous pot but could see no sign of her comrades, so she continued apologizing profusely as she bowed and scraped her way back towards the gate. The three of us had ducked down beneath the hedge and we were now all desperately holding on to our mouths and noses trying not to make any sound as we stared at each other in wide-eyed disbelief. This was better than *Dallas*.

'My dear woman.' Presumably this was the hostess, the one in the regal silver gown, now addressing Julia in a lecturing tone. 'If you had wanted to use the bathroom, you had only to knock on the door. We are not savages, you know.'

'Actually, madam, I'm delivering a pissagram,' purred Julia as she spotted us all crouching down by the pavement, 'and you now have the choice of a poem or a song.'

★　★　★

As the taxi pulled up into a side alley, I noticed a small excitable crowd gathered outside the dingy hole-in-the-wall entrance to the club, all being herded behind barriers by two Tysonesque bouncers.

'Follow me,' said Julia as we stepped out of the cab, and she took my hand while the others kept close to heel. She nodded at the burly man with the headset and microphone. He nodded back at her, chewed on his gum and pulled up the heavy red rope that stood between the revellers and their ultimate prize of a heaving dance floor beyond. Pushing people out of the way to create a path, he then motioned Julia an all-clear wave and we were swept right in. The receptionist saw Julia then waved to one of the greeters to come and escort us. Julia blew her a kiss and then looked around to make sure that we were all still together. She smiled at me and said, 'Ready?'

'I was born ready,' said Sara. And the doors to the inner sanctum of the club were opened to reveal a vision of utter hedonism. Thronging is just not the word. There were people everywhere, shouting loudly to be heard over the deafening music, standing on furniture to dance because they couldn't get to the floor, passing drinks above heads, and I swear I saw a man dressed as a skeleton dancing in a cage suspended from the ceiling.

We started to edge our way pushily through the crowd, the hostess looking over her shoulder now and again to check the crocodile behind her.

'We're in VIP!' shouted Sara by way of explanation to me and then again to Leoni. 'We're always in VIP! It's bloody great here!' and she put her hands high in the air and broke into her best funky moves as we continued our way through the heaving mass of bodies.

As we reached another bouncer-laden barrier, the pretty lady in the sari spoke to the head honcho with the dark glasses, turned around and pointed us out. Then she waved us goodbye and disappeared back into the writhing crowd.

'This way, ladies.' The heavy motioned us through a curtain of richly embroidered wall hangings. Another goddess in a sari approached us and said, 'My name's Tracey and I'll be serving you tonight. Your table's this way.' And she showed us through an intimately sumptuous inner enclave to our own comfortably furnished naughty corner.

'What can I bring you to drink?' she said.

'Coffee?' asked Leoni hopefully.

Tracey looked sympathetically at the befuddled Leoni. 'You've come to the wrong place if you're looking for a cup of coffee, girl,' she laughed.

'Bring us a magnum,' Julia said. 'And Sara, this time, don't try any of that shit with the straw, okay?'

Sara laughed apologetically before her ears pricked up to the banging bassline now pouring through from the room beside us.

'Who wants to dance?' She was already pulling Leoni out of her seat and it seemed pointless to argue with her. 'Come on!' she urged, and we left our belongings under our seats and made for the noise.

It'd been several years and a whole lot more since I shook my thang, and judging by the eye-popping gyrations among the scantily clad minors on the podiums, I was going to have to make do with looking decidedly old hat. Not a handbag in sight. Nor a bra for that matter. I did my best to go with the flow and opted for a Chaka Khan rooted-to-the-spot Seventies Diva style. It felt pretty good actually, so I let the martinis take the moment and went for a full-on disco spin.

Spurred on by this spontaneous move, Leoni leaped in front of me and did a *Pulp Fiction* Jack Rabbit Flash in a moment of pure Uma Thurman inspiration. She then scambled onto a table, much to the surprise of its seated occupants, and broke into a highly animated mashed potato. Her table audience egged her on, clapping their hands and punching the air around her, and that's when it happened.

Leoni and I had done ballet together at school for a while. She had always been much better than me, her willowy undeveloped body lending itself beautifully to Miss Marshall's idea of Bolshoi perfection. She was good, but not that good, and as we had pointed out to her more than once, it's easy to look like Margot Fonteyn when you're surrounded by a classroom full of galumphing crisp munchers. She now saw her moment to shine, and threw herself into a monumental high kick of Parisian proportions.

Fifteen years and three children on from her last dance class, the strain proved too much for her depleted body, which now clear left the table and landed with a spectacular crash in the gap between it and the laps of the stunned cinema-goers.

'Housewife down!' screamed Sara, hands cupped around her mouth to create the makeshift megaphone with which she now addressed the entire club.

I haven't enjoyed myself so much in years.

CHAPTER 7

LAND THIS THING!

The receptionists arming the front desk of the beauty salon were scarcely able to mask their disgust at the sight of the en-masse appointment as we trundled in through the heavy glass doors. Had we survived a plane crash and then walked all the way there from the Alps we would have looked better, and I was becoming increasingly aware that the cold shower and extra splash of perfume was now doing little to disguise the alcoholic fumes rising out of my every pore. I felt utterly appalling and wished that someone would come along and put me out of my misery with a single well-aimed silver bullet.

Julia approached the painted lady with the perfectly manicured hands, lifted her wide dark glasses and perched them on the top of her pounding head.

'We have an appointment,' she said.

The four stylists had their work cut out for them that morning. Sara got the only man, although I use the term advisedly, and he visibly recoiled when Sara turned to face him as we were shown to our seats. I wasn't surprised. She was still sporting most of last night's make-up, but not all of it, and not necessarily where she'd applied it, and she had point-blank refused to get into the shower that morning saying that her hair hurt and she would be sick if we forced her to wash.

Instead, she had ordered a monstrous breakfast from room service which arrived ceremoniously on a trolley-cum-table, had taken one bite, and then rolled onto the floor saying that she didn't want it. So we all had a little go at it in turns over the hour or two it took us to drag ourselves out of bed, until eventually every morsel was gone. It's amazing how thrifty one can get when sobering up to the price of a five-star sausage.

Now Julia ordered us all a smoothie. That's a drink. Not a person. And we sat and eyed the stylists as they became increasingly flustered at being handed such an onerous task on a Saturday morning.

'What the hell are you doing?' demanded Leoni as she watched the sides of her hair being blow-dried into the shape of a satellite dish. 'You're making me look like a chicken!'

'Well how do you want it?' pleaded the ex-asperated bearer of the dryer.

'Just NORMAL,' boomed Leoni. 'Oh for God's sake, give me the dryer and I'll do it myself.' A small scuffle broke out as Leoni became unreasonable and the stylist refused to hand over her power tool, and we all had to gang up on Leoni and more or less force her to retake her seat.

'She's on,' explained Sara to a red-faced Vidal.

'Sara!' gasped Leoni.

'So,' said Julia, ignoring the deliberate bitching and finally getting straight to the point. 'What did you think of Dudley and his friend, then?'

All eyes turned to me.

Dudley and his friend, whose name I cannot recall for the life of me, had joined us briefly during the tail end of our soirée the night before. To be honest, I hadn't heard a word of the conversation, and when Dudley asked me just as we were leaving whether I'd like to join him for a drink one evening, I really hadn't realized what he was saying until he pressed his telephone number into my hand. I had hoped that no one else had noticed, but I could see from Julia's expression that I hadn't got away with it.

'Well I don't really know,' I replied. 'I only met him for a minute and I couldn't hear a word of what went on, so I really don't think I should be passing comment on someone I don't know at all.' I feigned indifference.

'He's good looking,' said Leoni.

'Yeah. And he paid our bill,' chipped in Sara as she looked into her smoothie and pulled a face.

'So?' pressed Julia.

'So what?' I pretended to look at the magazine in my lap.

106

'So are you going to call him?'

'Certainly not!' I said indignantly. 'Good grief, Julia. I've not been widowed more than five minutes and you're trying to set me up with the nearest available man before the ink's even dry on the death certificate.' The stylists suddenly looked a lot less bored, and I could see them exchanging glances and leaving the blow-drying a little longer so they could hear how the story turned out.

Julia arched an eyebrow. 'He's nice.' She winked at me. 'And he's got a good healthy lawyer's wallet, and no one's suggesting here that you should marry him. He's a confirmed bachelor anyway. Far too rich to get married. Just go out and have a bit of fun! What's wrong with that?'

'You seem to know an awful lot about this Dudley all of a sudden,' I said.

'Just enough to get by,' Julia said with a wry smile.

'Well I'm not ringing him, and that's all there is to it.'

'That's okay,' Julia replied, turning her attention back to the outrageously sculptural male model draped achingly across the full-page advertisement in her magazine. 'I gave him your number. Told him you were a bit shy. He did seem pretty keen. You must have made an impression.'

The banter rose to an excitable level once more and the dryers blew in unison and set the tone for the rest of the day. As the last hairs were teased into place and sprayed triumphantly into position,

Sara dramatically pulled the gown from her shoulders, tossed her now perfect locks and fixed a vixenly stare on her terrified hairdresser.

'Bet you fancy me now,' she said.

By the time I got home late in the afternoon, the enormous lunch I had steadfastly trawled my way through had induced in me an advanced state of acute food coma, and the only thing now preventing me from slipping into a deep vegetative state was the thought of being able to sit in front of the television anytime soon nursing a warm glass of hot chocolate. Alas, it was not to be. I should have been more vigilant. As the taxi pulled up in front of the house I didn't notice Sheila's car loitering with intent outside the next-door neighbour's, and by the time I had, she was already locked on target and heading my way. I would have sent the driver around the block a couple of times had I been quicker off the mark; now I found myself an unsuspecting volunteer in an all-new episode of *Endurance*.

'Helen!' she called. 'Well talk about perfect timing! I thought I'd missed you!'

'Hello, Sheila.'

'To be honest,' she conspired, 'I thought you might not be answering the door so I went round to the back and had a good old look to make sure you weren't hanging from the rafters.'

'Thanks,' I said.

'Ooh, I do like your hair! Have you just had it

done? Oh yes,' she continued, walking around behind me and assessing the back. 'Very brave! You must tell me who you went to. Was it local? I could do with a bit of a makeover myself.'

Sheila has the kind of hair which has looked exactly the same for thirty years. Even in her school photographs, there it is. Sheila's hair. In her bid to keep it precisely the same colour and volume over the latter half of her lifetime, she must have subjected it to more chemicals than ICI's annual output, and it had long ago taken on a frighteningly fragile acrylic Barbie doll sheen. It's only a matter of time before someone lights a cigarette just that bit too close to her head and the whole thing disappears in one enormous pyrotechnic flash. A French pleat flambé, set off beautifully with a slick of coral lipstick in a blink of frosted-green eye shadow.

'Would you like a coffee?' I asked, when what I actually wanted to say was 'Why don't you just get into your hag wagon right now and sod off back to Stepford?'

But I didn't. I'm not like that.

As I sat there listening to her droning on and on and rapidly losing the will to live, the doorbell went. Hallelujah. Praise the Lord.

'Julia!' Having left her just a couple of hours ago, she was the last person I was expecting to see. My prayer had been answered.

'Recognize anything?' Julia held up my make-up

bag in front of my eyes and raised her eyebrows expectantly. 'You left your face in my bag. And your hair. And your red dress.'

I wasn't surprised. I had felt so ghastly as we checked out of the hotel that I would gladly have left everything behind rather than deal with the Herculean feat of packing. I couldn't have organized my way out of a paper bag. I apologized for being a useless particle.

'Don't mention it.' Julia started heading back towards her car.

I reached to grab her coat sleeve.

'No! Julia! You have to come in!' I whispered loudly. She frowned at me. I pulled the front door up close to the latch so that I wouldn't be heard by Attila.

'It's that bloody Sheila!' I said. 'She's been in my kitchen for over an hour and if you don't come in and rescue me I'm going to have to kill her and bury her body under the patio and then spend the rest of my life being someone's bitch in Holloway.'

Julia eyed the front door with a gritty look of resolve and I returned to the kitchen proudly with my impressive reinforcement.

'Oh how nice!' started Sheila.

'Hi, Shirley,' said Julia. 'Still persevering with that antiquarian husband of yours?' Julia switched the kettle on and Sheila clearly didn't understand the question.

'It's Sheila,' corrected the stunned Sheila. 'I was

just explaining to Helen that Graham and I have been saying that she really ought to think about getting out a little.'

Julia and I exchanged a hungover glance.

'So I went to the adult education centre at the college to see if they were running any more of those pottery evening classes you used to go to, didn't I, Helen?' Sheila was now rummaging about in her handbag.

'It's in here somewhere. Oh yes, here we are!' and she pulled a cheap green leaflet out from among her many important task lists and waved it towards me.

'The woman on reception wasn't very helpful, I have to say,' Sheila confided. 'She tried to tell me that they don't do arts and crafts courses there.' She raised her eyebrows and half closed her eyes to confirm how good she was at spotting a lie when she saw one. 'Absolute rubbish of course.' She shook her head as she dismissed the red herring. 'Anyway, I couldn't find any pottery classes so I thought I'd bring you the prospectus so that you can see if there's something else you fancy doing. I could come with you! Wouldn't that be nice?'

Somebody get me out of here.

'Pottery?' laughed Julia. 'You?' And she was genuinely taken aback at the thought that her little sister might have been whiling her sad little evenings away trying to learn how to throw a lump of soggy mud onto a spinning wheel and turn it into something practical. Like a noose.

'I really don't think so,' I said to Sheila, shaking my head and smiling politely.

'But you can't just sit around here grieving forever!' insisted Sheila. 'And we never did get to see anything that you made.'

'It was all pretty terrible,' I explained, 'so I never brought any of it home.'

Julia was still looking highly amused at the disclosure but now started to manoeuvre Sheila out of the kitchen.

'Oh will you look at that?' she said. 'No more tea. And no coffee either! Well it must be time to leave, then. Anyway, it was nice to see you again, Shirley, and do give my regards to Gordon.'

'Sheila,' corrected Sheila again. 'And Graham.'

'Sorry,' said Julia without looking or sounding sorry at all. The chill she had managed to place in the air did the trick splendidly and Sheila soon reached for her jacket.

'I'll pop in and see you tomorrow,' said Sheila as I led her towards the door. I took a deep breath.

'I'd really rather you didn't,' I said. 'If that's okay with you,' I added quickly. 'It's just that I'm not sure whether I'll be here and I wouldn't want you to have a wasted journey like you almost did today.'

'Oh nonsense!' said Sheila, then seeing Julia heading towards the door, she beat a hasty retreat and sped away.

'If I ever end up like that, shoot me,' Julia said.

★ ★ ★

112

I devoted the rest of my evening to the television, paying close but squeamish attention to the cosmetic surgery disasters that flashed across the little screen, and I couldn't help but feel a huge surge of sympathy towards the women who paraded their hideous scars in front of the camera and claimed how their lives had been ruined by a scalpel-wielding Latvian who, it turned out, was barely qualified to carve a turkey. She would never have gone ahead with the operation had she known. What did we think she was? Stupid? And, as she said, how could she have checked his credentials for herself when he didn't speak a word of English? Well he didn't need to, did he? The photographs she had been shown were nothing short of miraculous, and the nice woman who spoke perfect English and had seen her during her assessment appointment in the hotel 'consulting room' had been very knowledgeable and professional.

One lady did a piece direct to camera under the encouraging eye of the fly on the wall, and issued a stern and rawly emotive warning to the viewers against taking out a home-improvement loan and then spending it on an EC tummy tuck. The audience all bent double and protected their abdomens with a sharp intake of breath as she lifted her jumper and displayed the carnage beneath. Bloody Norah, I thought, you mean tummy fuck, mate. And don't even get me started on that grandmother with her Frankenstein face-lift. She'd never make it through passport control again.

I slept on the sofa that night. It felt good.

For some reason I decided to have a go at the back of the oven on Monday morning to try to do something about the little bits of gunk that had welded themselves to the mesh in front of the fan. I suppose it was because I had become enthralled by the extraordinary story unfolding on *Woman's Hour* about an elderly Jamaican lady who had fostered dozens, if not hundreds, of kids throughout her adult life.

She was affectionately referred to by them all as Nanna Applebags, because her speciality for settling in her troubled charges was a plate loaded high with her special apple dumplings. From the sounds of the recipe, those things could stop a truck at forty paces. She talked affectionately about the times she had been bruised black and blue from the constant assaults from a squalling houseful of disturbed minors, and how each one of them had been taught that it was okay to feel angry, so long as they understood that it was a pathway in their life leading to better things.

I listened to her gently laughing voice as she talked about how, many years later, all of her surrogate children had kept in touch with her, in time bringing their own families to her, introducing her as their mother, and delivering to her the largest extended family ever known to womankind. Her energies and

114

love had known no boundaries. She was an angel from heaven, sent to rescue a sea of urchins, and her unshakeable devotion was a lesson to us all.

Then came the sting. During the years of self-lessness and dedication, she had overlooked the effects of her delinquent menagerie on her only child. A son she had named Thomas. Knowing how important that part of his mother's life was, Thomas had helped and supported her throughout the difficult years and learned that at the end of each long day there would be nothing left for him. She had always thought of Thomas as a shining beacon in her vocational life, mature beyond his years, and able to understand the role she had to play and to comprehend that the result was that he must share his mother with many.

He had turned to drugs at fifteen and she didn't even notice. Within a year, he was dead. Her voice still lilted with the soft calypso of her homeland, but now it was sad and wise about the one that got away.

I had to gather myself for a moment before answering the telephone.

'Mrs Robbins?' It was WPC Jane, calling to check I hadn't killed myself, I suspected. I didn't recognize her voice at first, so she politely identified herself and I returned instantly to the feelings I had had that awful afternoon when we'd first met.

'I wonder if I could drop by later on today?' she

continued. 'Just a couple of formalities that we need to clear up. Nothing too complicated. It really shouldn't take long.' She sounded apologetic.

'Of course,' I said.

'Oh yes, and I'll be bringing a Mr Carpenter with me. He's from one of the insurance companies that your husband had recently taken out a policy with. It's just a couple of routine questions, nothing to worry about.' Her tone was friendly.

'Yes of course,' I repeated, but my heart had picked up a couple of paces, and I immediately began to get that swelling feeling of anxiety again.

'Sugar?' I asked as I poured the freshly brewed coffee that I had stewed over since answering the door to my inquisitors.

'Two, please,' said Mr Carpenter as he tried to penetrate my thoughts in a Vulcan mind melt with no hands. Two sugars is excessive and greedy, I observed. Must be a jobsworth.

Now that the coffee was poured and the condimentary details attended to, there was nowhere left for me to hide. I thought about trying to squash myself into the cabinet under the television, but I don't think I would have got away with it. Besides, of the many things that I may be, a contortionist is not one of them. I tore my eyes away from the cabinet doors and smiled lamely at Jane.

'Mrs Robbins,' she began.

That's funny, I thought. I was Helen on Black Saturday, she was Jane, and now we're back to

Mrs Robbins and Constable. Did this mean I was under arrest? Or do you only get first-name treatment on Death Day?

'Please, do call me Helen.'

I didn't want to be arrested.

'Helen,' she corrected. 'Were you aware that shortly before the accident your husband took out a very large life insurance policy?'

'Did he?' I said.

'Yes. He did,' said Mr Carpenter.

'Oh.' I looked benignly at my coffee cup.

'Mrs Robbins,' Mr Carpenter was now fixed on my expression, 'can I ask you, do you know much about cars?'

'Not really,' I said vacuously.

'Mmm,' he said. 'They're pretty reliable these days, what with all the computerized gizmos and what have you, and the car manufacturers haven't been able to shed much light on why the airbags went off like that.' He took a rather uncouth swig from his cup. 'In fact, it's all a bit of a mystery.'

'I don't understand what you're saying,' I said. 'Are you suggesting that—'

'You see, the thing is . . .' Mr Carpenter was now drilling into my psyche with his special detective skill which is not of this world. 'When some-one comes to us and takes out a big life insur-ance policy, then that person dies in, well, shall we say unusual circumstances within a matter of weeks, it could be interpreted by some people –' he was waffling a bit, like when you see a senior policeman talking on the news outside the Old Bailey at the conclusion of some enormous trial '– as a little suspicious,' he finished sternly before slurping noisily from his coffee cup. Obviously more at home with a mug.

I looked at WPC Jane. What on earth was I supposed to say to something like that? She came to my rescue.

'Mrs Robbins, sorry, Helen. What Mr Carpenter means –' she gave him a sideways glance that had a certain sense of 'or else' about it '– what Mr Carpenter means is that they have some routine procedures to follow at a time like this.' She shot Mr Carpenter a core-freezing 'don't you dare' and continued.

'We all know that this is a tragic accident, Helen, but they just needed to send someone out to make sure that everything is in order.'

You mean, come over and check that I haven't got some twenty-year-old boy-band painter and decorator paying special attention to my architraves while I cash in the policies and rush out to buy some lurid underwear, I thought.

'Exactly.' Mr Carpenter, having broken rank in a moment of science-fiction fantasy and now finding himself beamed back into his physical reality as an insurance assessor, picked up the black briefcase he had brought with him, placed it on his lap, opened it up and pulled out a clear plastic wallet. He then made some lengthy ritual out of producing and laying out three forms, all of which

118

required a great amount of filling in on his part, and some degree of signing on mine. It became clear pretty quickly that he could have filled most of them in himself before he came, but I think that would have diminished the importance of his role, and he wouldn't have liked that at all. Jane looked at me once or twice during the form-handling masterclass and raised her eyes to the heavens with a little Mona Lisa smile. She really was as nice as I had remembered. If a little butch.

As I signed away the last of his doubts, Mr Carpenter packed the papers into his little plastic wallet, theatrically placed them back into his briefcase, stood up, and offered me his hand by way of a 'no hard feelings I was just doing my job' peace offering. I stood up and accepted the handshake.

And there it was. The wet wibble. If this man was already pretty low down in my estimation, he now sank without a trace. Julia had told me about the wet wibble years ago.

'Do men think that our hands will disintegrate in the face of an honest, firm handshake?' she had ranted. 'If there's one thing I can't stand, it's those men who shake a woman's hand using their thumb and first two fingers because they can't get their head around greeting and meeting us the same way as they would a man. Fight it or fuck it. That's their dilemma.' She pointed at the air. 'And if they want to fuck it, they can't possibly shake hands with it first.' I loved listening to Julia when she was on her high horse about something. 'It pisses me off so much that I now make a point of cracking a man's knuckles and bringing him to his knees when he first meets me. That way, we all know where we stand.'

Waving my official visit off from the front doorstep, I made a mental note to call Julia and ask her what exactly Sara had taken to her solicitor and whether it wasn't time for me to go and meet this legal eagle of hers. As I held that thought, I heard a strange electronic ringing sound, and after an initial spasm of stupidity, realized that it was my groovy new mobile. I really must try not to look like an idiot every time it rang. I intended to be popular.

'Hello?' I enquired, not having had a name flash up on the mini screen.

'Well hello there,' came the hair-raisingly charming voice.

I froze.

'Is that the very lovely Helen? Sister of Julia? Seeker of Bee Gee disco hits?' he asked. Now I knew who it was. This had to be Dudley. The one with the written references from my big sister.

'Dudley,' I said, 'how sweet of you to call.'

'Not a bit of it!' he responded. 'I've tried not thinking about you, but I'm really not doing a very good job of it, so I wondered if you would put me out of my misery and let me take you out to dinner one evening?' He spoke with an easy manner, and I found myself blushing on the other end of the telephone and wishing I had put some make-up on.

'Well . . . I don't know, Dudley, I . . .'

'Oh come on, Helen!' He pretended to be injured. 'I promise to be on my best behaviour.'

'Well, as I said, I . . .'

'And I know that you're not into dating or anything like that, but your sister seems to think that I'm the perfect escort to take you out for an inaugural airing.'

'Oh,' I said. 'So Julia's called you, has she?'

That was just typical. Here was me thinking that this bloke really had been distracted for days thinking about how nice it would be to take me out for dinner, and that he had had to muster his very best and pluck up the courage to call me and face the possibility of rejection, and that he had finally decided to rise to the occasion because he could not live another day without seeing me, and it turned out that he was under instructions from my sister. Great.

'Julia? No,' he said. 'Why, did she tell you she was going to call me?'

'Well no, I just thought . . .' I trailed off spectacularly.

'So.' He picked up the dead end of conversation. 'What about it, then? Say, Saturday at eight? I'll pick you up?'

I was smiling, and I felt silly.

'That would be lovely,' I said.

★ ★ ★

'Well, someone's looking radiant!' said Julia as she answered her door to me.

'Now don't you start.' I smiled back at her, pointing at her face and daring her to challenge me.

'So, where's he taking you?'

'I don't know,' I said, 'but what I do know is that it's a double-date with that friend of his whose name I still can't remember, and it's six o'clock instead of eight, so he must be desperate to spend an extra two hours with me.'

Julia smiled broadly and we both broke into an excited giggling fit, shoving each other around so that we could vent some of the mounting excitement that was starting to do my head in. I felt like an overemotional fourteen-year-old preparing to meet the destiny of her first snog. And I didn't even fancy Dudley. It was the prospect of being taken out for dinner that I had fallen head over heels in love with. How glitteringly crass.

'So what are you going to wear?' asked Julia.

'This!' I announced, and pulled a cloud of silk from the carrier bag I had brought with me. Julia let out a low whistle.

'Bloody hell,' she said. 'I hope you've joined a gym.'

When Saturday arrived, I spent the day like a teenager preparing for an illicit party. I unplugged the house phone (over the last week I'd realized that no one interesting called on that phone anyway) and surrendered myself to a day of primping, pampering and plucking. I drew the line at waxing, but only after having experienced the white-knuckle ride of a hastily abandoned torture-yourself-at-home kit. I retreated to the safety of a couple of cucumber slices placed restfully on the eyes.

Everything I used that day was new. That was strangely important to me, as though not wanting to contaminate the promise of something innocent and pure with anything tainted, like not wanting to use an old wooden spoon to stir the freshly made custard. As I opened each of the new cosmetics and potions that I had treated myself to while out with Julia but then hidden deep inside the wardrobe, I found myself reading all the little leaflets inside the boxes and even checking the *mode d'emploi* before applying the cream. I mean, who on earth needs instructions before rubbing on a bit of face cream? It was sad, I know.

Now ready to face my judge and jury, I stood in front of the full-length mirror and assessed my chances. I hardly recognized myself. As I stood there and tried to reacquaint Helen with the woman who stared back at me anxiously, I heard Robert's voice jeering at my new Bobbi Brown lipstick, and nervously adjusted my dress.

Who was I kidding? I looked ridiculous. I reached for a tissue to wipe off the lipstick and picked up my mobile as I rehearsed my last-minute.com excuse in my head. The sound of a car horn blaring loudly outside in the street broke my concentration. Too late. My knight in shining armour raised his hand in a wave from the open-air comfort of his shiny car towards the window I wish I hadn't appeared at.

'You look good enough to eat,' he pronounced as he opened the passenger side door for me and stood aside.

I stepped in as elegantly as I could given the kerb-brushing situation of the seat, and the smell of the soft hide cladding mingled with the expensive manly fragrance that he had probably researched before investing in. He jogged youthfully around to his side and leaped in before turning over the engine with a Bengali purr.

I couldn't restrain the smile of excitement that settled on my face.

'Ready for an adventure?' he called above the noise of his wild acceleration. I looked at him and laughed as I tried to control my flying hair and hoped that all the neighbours were watching.

As we reached the metropolis, the day began to fade and the street lights commenced the business of easing us beneath a deep, cobalt blanket of colourful, artificial stars. The music playing from the warmth of the doors lifted my spirits and I lay back in the cocoon of my seat, tilting my head upwards to see and absorb the glory that could only be London by night. Dudley turned and gave me a smile every now and again, and looked entirely at ease as he enjoyed his drive and delighted in the consummate comfort of his new acquaintance.

'Not far now!' he said as we neared the river. 'We're meeting Neil and his girlfriend there,' he called out without looking up from the road. 'I can't remember her name. I don't suppose he can either.' He laughed. And a couple of minutes later we turned into the parking lot of the heliport.

Now, up until that point, I had always prided myself on being one of those people who is not impressed by superficial, material nonsense. But at no time do I remember that that also included being taken to Paris in a helicopter for dinner. No, I think I'm safe on that one.

'Hello!' squealed the girlfriend as she tottered towards us and tried hopelessly to keep her newly acquired breasts from spilling out of the microchip that someone had obviously told her was a dress.

'My name's Dawn!' she bubbled, and she thrust her hand towards me and shook mine hard before planting a kiss on my cheek.

'Helen!' I shouted back and nodded hello as my hair now yielded to the supercharged mistral being kicked up by the waiting helicopter.

We abandoned any attempt at verbal communication as we were ushered to the aircraft and pointed towards our seats. Neil was already buckled up and gave me a thumbs-up greeting as Dudley settled me in. Headsets were passed around and we put them on and fastened our seat belts. A man standing outside on the tarmac did a big winding-up gesture with his hand high above his head, and I heard the engines switch from a thudding tick-over to a whining roar and we lifted effortlessly into the air.

I watched the ground below as it pulled away from us, and marvelled at the feeling of literal elation as the colourful lights once above us in the car now twinkled cheekily below as we gained height and banked away from the buildings.

Suddenly, I was deafened by a white noise screaming through my headphones. I turned from the window to see Dawn tearing at her seat belt, her face deranged with fear, lashing out at the boyfriend and screaming, 'Land! Fucking land! Land this thing right now!' and a terrible smell permeated the entire cabin.

Dudley was desperately trying to force Dawn back into her seat, and the pilot immediately switched to vox, saying in his calm zero-one-niner way, 'Get back into your seat, madam. I really must insist you sit down and fasten your seat belt imme-diately.' Dawn was now crying and screaming hysterically, flailing around dangerously in the aircraft, trying to strangle the boyfriend and constantly yelling, 'Land! Now! Fucking land!'

By now, her pashmina was caught up in some kind of significant knob (no, not his) and the pilot was worryingly calling, 'Mayday! Mayday!' and we started heading downwards with the kind of purchase that makes the high-speed lift in the

Empire State Building feel like a Noddy car. It was one hell of a time for Dawn to find out she suffered from vertigo, and in those few interminable minutes I had a hell of a time myself preparing to go to that big supermarket in the sky.

The ground crew were ready and waiting for us as the pilot touched down onto the big H, and Dawn was physically removed, still crying and shaking hysterically, by the man with the orange table-tennis bats and his bemused sidekick who usually had to do little more than check the occasional suspicious barking hand luggage.

'Are you all right?' asked Dudley as the engine noise wound down and he helped me out of the flying circus.

'I think so,' I said as lightly as I could.

The fact was, that had been one major trippy experience and I was feeling just the wrong side of nauseous. Correction. I was going to throw up and there was absolutely nothing I could do about it. So I did. Right there and then.

Oh well. I didn't want to have his kids anyway.

CHAPTER 8

GRIEF

I t's a funny thing, grief.

It can come winging in at you from out of nowhere and cut you down at the knees when you're least expecting it. I had really thought that I was doing all right. In the few weeks that had passed since Robert's death, I had pretty much gone through the full spectrum of emotions. Shock, for definite, as I tried to get a handle on the fact that he was gone for good. Anxiety, big time, every time I found myself either losing my already tenuous grip on reality, or waking up in a cold sweat in the middle of the night, vividly dreaming that he was still there, my life un-changed, still walking on eggshells and spending most of my mental energies trying to side-step his unreasonable behaviour. And then there was the guilt of course. In spades.

In amongst those terrible nightmares were other dreams too. Dreams about how things might otherwise have been. It was like entering a parallel universe where my life turned out completely differently. The blood-red velvet curtains would be raised to a silken overture and I would sit back in wonder, watching this extraordinary play, seeing myself there so happy, with an adoring husband at my side, surrounded by beautiful children, hands linked together in a ring-a-roses of family love. It was sunshine in every possible way. The dream would stay with me all morning, and I wondered if that could have been my life had I tried a little harder. After all, what are dreams if not doorways to other realities?

Today I had finally decided to tackle some of the tasks I had been putting off. Such had been my trepidation at the prospect of going through Robert's belongings that I had left it almost immediately each time I resolved to begin. I couldn't bring myself to make it all feel that real, but each time I met one of his artefacts as I moved around the house, my feelings of worry would rise swiftly, so I concluded that I really had no choice other than to put everything of Robert's out of sight, out of mind.

I went into the spare room where Robert kept all his clothes – there had never been enough room in the minuscule built-in wardrobes in the marital bedroom – and I opened up his closet. There inside were all the shirts which I had ironed a fortnight ago, regardless of the fact that there was no longer anyone to wear them. They lined up in front of me expectantly, fresh and untouched. I took out the one with the pink stripes that I had bought for him the previous Christmas. It still had the label on. It was the same make as the ones he used to wear in our younger days before the mortgage had dictated he switch to a more modest brand. He had asked whether I had got him the matching cravat and said something about it coming in handy if he were ever to decide to dance on the other side of the fence.

There was a suit carrier pushed right to the far end of the rail. I pulled it out and rested it on the bed while I unzipped the cover. It was his wedding suit. I touched the beautiful deep-blue light-wool fabric and lifted one of the arms to my cheek. It smelled very faintly of the aftershave he used to wear. I slipped the whole thing out of the cover and took the trousers off the hanger. It was smaller than his suits now. Less generous in the cut, slimmer on the waist. I checked the empty pockets before folding the trousers again neatly.

Then I reached up for the pile of jumpers on the top shelf above the rail and pulled them all down. I re-folded each one carefully and set it onto the pile with the wedding suit, including the two identical black and tan diamond-pattern golf sweaters which had had to be kept clean and rotated at all times in case the opportunity of an unexpected round with the boss came up.

As I continued to take out his clothes and bag them up for the charity shop, I couldn't help but notice how much stuff he had and what he must have been spending on his appearance while I was left to siphon off a miserly pittance by asking for cashback at the local supermarket and slipping the notes into the gap I had niftily created by slitting and hemming the lining of my handbag on the part hidden underneath the side compartment. A nice lady I got talking to at the bus stop one day had given me that tip.

Wardrobe finally empty, I looked at the dusty corners and went to the kitchen to get the washing-up bowl and a squirt of detergent. I have always found something comforting in the ritual of cleaning. That moment when you snap on the rubber gloves and determine to wash away the grime that's craftily collected in the places you haven't been looking. The satisfaction of scrubbing away at an innocent face of gloss paint, watching the water turn a muddy grey and greeting the feeling of achievement with a certain sense of self-worth. Days I've spent doing that. And nobody's ever noticed.

I went to answer the doorbell.

'Helen? I hope I'm not disturbing you.' It was Mrs Henderson from next door but one. We don't know each other really, except to exchange keys once a year in case the house tries to burn itself down while one of us is away on holiday.

'Carol! Hello,' I said.

She's a nice lady, from the little I know of her. Always gives a polite wave and a smile if we see each other in the street.

She had a pretty bunch of roses in her hand.

They were obviously from her garden, because they were proper roses, like little pale cabbages, and they smelled divine. She had clearly sacrificed the best of her precious blooms. You couldn't buy roses like that if you searched the world for a month of Sundays. She held them towards me.

'I've been thinking about you since I heard the dreadful news about your husband, and I just wanted to let you know that if there is anything I can do to help, you mustn't hesitate for a moment.'

I took the little foil-wrapped posy and marvelled at the beauty of each bursting head of porcelain petals.

'Oh Carol, they're beautiful.' And I held them up to my nose and let their perfume fill my head and push away the cloying stench of guilt and charity bags.

'Will you come in?' I stepped aside and hoped that she would.

'Oh, no,' she said, looking embarrassed and shaking her hands in front of her in a mini Olympian-winner's wave. 'I really didn't want to impose on you. I just wanted to let you know that, well . . .' Her shoulders relaxed. 'We've been neighbours for a long time, Helen, and what else are neighbours for?'

I looked back at the flowers in my hand and thought at that moment that I was going to cry. I thought of Carol out in her garden, inspecting her roses, secateurs in hand, choosing only the best of her pride, cutting each one down and hoping that their beauty wouldn't be wasted on the woman she hardly knew.

'Carol, I'd be so grateful to share a bit of company at the moment,' I said.

She looked at me with compassion and stepped inside.

Dear Mrs Henderson from number forty-six stayed with me for the whole of the afternoon, and when she left, she insisted on taking the Robert bags with her, backing her car into the driveway and filling every available space with the bin liners into which we had together decanted the last vestiges of his presence. She had been firm and ruthless in her resolve to stop me pondering the history of each item, telling me not to think about it and to send it away if it made me feel bad. She didn't ask me any questions, and offered to make tea whenever I looked like I was flagging, which by my reckoning was every hour, on the hour. At the end of our long, physical afternoon, I had found the piles of black plastic bags horribly upsetting. A huge mountain of body bags filled with severed heads and limbs. All Robert's.

I poured myself an unapologetically enormous brandy and sat down at the kitchen table.

And the tears came in like a tidal wave.

'What you need is a holiday,' concluded Leoni as she heaved load number fifteen of the world laundry mountain out of her washing machine.

'Oh bloody bollocks,' she cursed as she pulled murky pink sheet after murky pink sheet into the waiting plastic basket. She spun the empty drum round in search of the criminal and there, wedged evilly against the rim, was the offending red football shirt. She peeled it away from the big steel colander and swore at it, before loading the wet sheets back into the machine and searching on the utility shelves for the multi-pack of washing-accident white-restorer sachets. Leoni tore one open and threw it into the machine before switching it on again. 'I hate it when that happens,' she said before turning her attentions back to me.

'Why don't you go to a health farm?' she suggested. 'I'd love that. Swanning around all day in a free dressing gown with matching slippers and being given a good old rub down by some Australian sports therapist with a bottle of lavender-infused oil.' She shot me a wicked smile as she imagined being manhandled by a surf dude with a confident, if presumptuous, touch.

My holidays until now had mainly consisted of spending long, boringly hot days trying to find some way to occupy myself in a hotel in the middle of nowhere in Portugal, while Robert went off and did his thing for hours on end and I found myself stranded on campus with a highly strung community of golf widows. They seemed to go to an awful lot of trouble with their looks considering their husbands were unlikely to put in an appearance until way after sundown, and their conversation, always sounding a little too close to hysteria, was largely centred around 'What does your husband do?' before launching into details about their spectacularly successful spouses, houses, cars and shopping allowances. I was often tempted to answer the staple opening question with 'He's a senior wanker. What about yours?'

'I don't think so.' I laughed. The thought of joining a full legion of sad, insecure women and incurably fat rich people was not something that I was in the least bit tempted to research, book and, worst of all, pay for.

But apart from her fantasy, Leoni had pretty much hit the nail on the head. I was feeling more claustrophobic than ever, as though I wanted to punch everybody out of my way and break into a full-on sprint to run far from here and burn off some of the loose-cannon adrenalin that was coursing relentlessly through my veins.

'Well what do you fancy, then?' asked Leoni.

'Oh I don't know,' I conceded. 'I'd just like to get a change of scenery for a while, you know, get a different perspective on things, get away from all this.' I gestured at nothing. 'See somewhere new.'

I imagined myself drifting aimlessly on a sleek and eye-catching yacht, raising my face to the Mediterranean sun as I relaxed on deck, lost in lofty thoughts as the boat swayed gently on the swell of a turquoise sea, undisturbed by the taut-T-shirted crew as they raised full sail and pointed the bow into the sunset. I looked fabulous, *naturellement*.

Leoni and I indulged ourselves in the speculation of wildly romantic holiday situations and weighed up the possibilities of a world cruise before her kitchen timer went off and pushed her towards the reality of the school run. After my last encounter with the sabotage twins, I saw this as my cue to leave. Must try to do something about that other-people's-kids thing. It can't be good karma.

'Start spreading the news!' sang Julia loudly as she burst in through the front door some days later. All these years on, I had finally managed to return the favour by presenting Julia with her own key.

'We,' she announced dramatically, 'are going to strip Fifth Avenue of anything that doesn't have an Ebola contamination sticker on it.' And she sprang into her version of a New York street hip-hop breaker and spun into the kitchen, depositing a brochure on the table before snapping on the kettle.

'New York?' I repeated.

'Yep. New Bloody York. The city that doesn't sleep.' She deposited herself in the chair opposite me at the kitchen table.

'Oh,' I said.

This was a bit of a bolt from the blue. I had been thinking a little more coconuts and palm trees than that myself, but had got no further than flicking through a few brochures, eventually becoming so depressed at searching through the jargon for the single-supplement information that I had given it all up as a bad job. My new strategy was to take advantage of something that had already been thought about for me. Like the full-page advertisements in the weekend-supplement magazines. All I had to do was find one that I liked and Bob would almost certainly become my uncle. But everything I had seen so far had a definite ring of couples about it, apart from the terrifyingly jolly specialist singles trips, and both would be far too awful for words. I didn't want to spend my 'finding myself' holiday finding myself fighting off widowers, or other people's husbands, or indeed their wives, rather as I had done with Graham and Sheila lately.

Graham had taken to popping in unexpectedly just a bit too often recently. Always freshly showered – evident from his damp hair – and shrouded in a gaggingly excessive fog of duty-free cologne, he had become increasingly difficult to persuade away from the doorstep, and I had wondered on more than one occasion whether I should approach Julia and ask her to headhunt for me a fat-necked bouncer from one of her many late-night haunts. The penny dropped well and truly when Sheila started popping in with clock-setting reliability about half an hour after Graham had made an appearance. On one such occasion, I was almost certain that she had a rolling pin, or perhaps a Kalashnikov, tucked under her raincoat, and she actually refused my offer of coffee which was so out of the ordinary that I considered calling an ambulance for her.

She was following him, I realized. And if she was following him, she must have been thinking that she was going to find a crock at the end of his clandestine rainbow. A crock of what, I don't know, but it certainly didn't include me. Between you and me, I think that my new-found free status had ruffled a few well-settled feathers here and there. There's nothing like a sniff of perfectly seared prime steak to bring out the vampire in the most confirmed of vegetarians, and the garnish of a not-quite-past-her-amuse-by-date widow with her own house and a couple of quid in the bank seemed to be the perfect Béarnaise.

I thought of New York and the prospect of sailing around Saks and sipping Manhattans in Manhattan.

'Have you already booked it?' I hid behind my tea cup.

'No,' Julia replied as she scrutinized one of the conditions in the small print. 'Sara's just checking availability and trying to clear next Friday and Monday in my diary. I thought we could go for a long weekend.' She was concentrating on the brochure and trying to find the page she had settled on as the best place in town.

'Would you mind if I said I'd rather not?' I said quietly.

'What?' she said, looking up sharply from the page she had finally found.

'Julia.' I sighed and put my hands through the front of my hair. 'I've not been feeling too great these last couple of weeks and I really think that I need to take some time out and be alone.'

It was the nearest I had got to saying No in many, many years. I waited for the world to end. For the sky to fall in around my ears. But it didn't. I had to remember to breathe.

'Oh Helen, I am so sorry,' said Julia. 'God. Here's me crashing around and making assumptions about you and I hadn't even stopped to look.' She came and sat right next to me.

'Are you okay?' she asked.

'I don't know,' I said, and I started crying again.

Julia put her arm around my shoulders and reached across the table to get a tissue out of her bag. I dried my eyes and blew my nose. I felt wretched.

'Look,' said Julia as she took a pen and a business card out of her handbag. 'There's this brilliant guy I know. He's not a therapist, but he kind of is, if you see what I mean.' She started writing his name and number on the back of the card. 'I had a serious crash and burn a few years ago,' she continued as she handed me the card. 'And this chap helped me through it. I don't know how he did it, but what I do know is that every time I went and talked to him I came out feeling a hell of a lot better.'

I looked at her. Julia seeing a therapist? Now I'd heard it all.

'I still see him,' she finished earnestly with a little nod. 'I think I would go mad if I didn't.' She put the pen back in her bag and placed the card in front of me.

'Call him,' she said. 'What have you got to lose?'

It took me nearly a week to pluck up the courage to make the call. In the end it was hardly my own decision. I had become so emotionally unstable, crying at the moving sight of the fresh vegetables in the supermarket, breaking down while watching *EastEnders* and that kind of thing, that I really had no choice other than to get some help. I rang Julia first to try to get some more information but she refused to tell me anything about him and said I should just go with an open mind and take from it whatever I wanted to.

In my mind's eye I had built this Timothy bloke into a chanting kaftan-wearing weirdo and imagined myself being made to sit under a makeshift pyramid set up in his spare bedroom, so when I rang the doorbell of his Kensington house I was taken aback by the sight of a gentle-looking man in his early fifties nicely turned out in a pair of fawn corduroy trousers and a cotton shirt with a pale blue sweater knotted carelessly around his shoulders.

'You must be Helen. Tim Hopkins,' he said, and

e before showing me into

',' he said, and he led me
wall filled with wonderful
nily photographs. I tried
[followed closely behind
ear nosey. The wallpaper

: all right?' he said as he
ntimate wood-panelled
... the end of the hall.

'Yes. No problem at all,' I said. 'In fact I had a lovely walk from the tube.'

The room smelled of years of lavender wood polish and well-worn books, with deeply patterned Eastern rugs warming the oak floor that looked as though it had been there since time began, and there was a silver tray set out with a pot of fresh coffee waiting on the small occasional table in the far corner.

'Coffee?' he asked.

'Yes please,' I said, still looking around and admiring the room. I didn't see any certificates on the wall, or a couch to lie and bleed on, and there was no sign at all of a pyramid. This was a gentleman's room. He poured the coffee slowly, taking his time and preparing each cup properly.

I started to feel terribly nervous. My hand shook as I attempted to take a sip of coffee, so I put the cup back onto the saucer as steadily as I could, trying to keep the rattling to a minimum, and carefully set it down on the edge of his desk. He was watching me quietly as he drank a little of his. I smiled now and again but nothing more came.

'So, Helen,' he began, 'what brings you here?'

He looked genuinely interested to hear the answer to his question, but I really didn't have the first idea where to start. When your whole world comes tumbling down, you are left with something like an earthquake scene. Rubble everywhere. The once familiar landscape changed beyond recognition in an instant. As you survey the sheer scale of the disaster, how can you walk into the devastation and pick up a single piece and say, 'This is the part that caused the entire city to collapse'?

'My husband was killed in an accident two months ago,' I said.

It was a sentence of such gravity that I couldn't possibly imagine how he could even begin to form an answer to the challenge of the day.

'I'm so sorry, Helen,' he said gently. 'That must have been very difficult for you.'

'Yes,' I said.

He didn't say anything more. Just sat there patiently and waited for me to continue. But I couldn't think of anything else to say, so I smiled again without conviction and held his sympathetic silence. He came to my assistance when the time-lapse edged towards awkwardness.

'Bereavement is a very powerful emotion,' he acknowledged, before allowing another pause in case I wanted to pick up the ball and run with it. I didn't.

'The grieving process can be very complicated. You know, in some cultures, grieving the dead can go on for years. Indeed it wasn't that long ago that in this country a bereaved spouse would wear mourning clothes for two whole years so that the outside world would know just by looking that they were suffering the long-term effects of a great loss.'

I nodded. He waited again before continuing.

'How's your day-to-day life at the moment, Helen?' he asked.

'Not good.' I smiled apologetically.

Oh no. Here come the tears again. He reached for the tissues that had been strategically placed on top of a pile of books by the desk and put the box next to me. I took a grateful handful and tried to get myself in order. He leaned forward and touched my arm so that I would look at him.

'Don't worry,' he reassured me quietly. 'Go ahead. This is all good. Honestly.' And he waited patiently while I sat there blubbering.

'You know, we're all different,' he said. 'We all handle things in different ways and come at life from different angles. It's perfectly normal that you should be feeling some deep emotions at this time. You're probably feeling very scared right now. It's okay to feel like that. You mustn't try to shut those feelings out.'

I nodded.

'And your late husband. I expect you miss him very much.'

I stopped crying and finished mopping my face.

'No,' I said to him bravely, looking him square in the eyes. 'I'm glad he's dead. He was a shit actually.' And I straightened my back and waited for the gasp of shock. There was not a flicker of reaction on Tim's face.

'That must be very hard for you.'

I stared at him. What?

'Did you ever wish him dead?' he asked. 'Guilt makes grieving much harder, you know.'

I felt my face flush a hot red and fiddled with the damp tissues in my hand.

'It's all right. You don't have to answer that.' He smiled and waved his question away.

I busied myself trying to pick up the coffee cup without upsetting the whole thing over the papers on the desk. I couldn't believe that I had just said that. My heart was pounding, and the rich dark coffee gave me a welcome moment of comfort.

Tim sat back in his chair and put down the pad he had been making notes in.

'You know, I meet a lot of people,' he started. 'Mostly men, in fact mostly very successful men.'

'Women?' I sniffled, knowing very well that Julia for sure was one.

'Very few, sadly,' he said. 'Women don't usually ask for help. They're too busy just getting on with it.'

He folded his arms and looked at me openly.

'The common thread that runs between them all is the loneliness of being a pioneer. What makes some people want to develop great ideas while others sit around and wonder why nothing so exciting ever happens to them?' Tim allowed me to ponder the question and then went on.

'The big difference with people who pursue their dreams and turn them into a great success, like that Dyson chap for instance, is a simple matter of belief.' I was listening intently. 'I'm not saying that hard work isn't involved, it's just that some people believe in their ideas so strongly that they will get up and do something about it, while others don't, and won't.' He had a soft voice and a perfect bedside manner. 'How many people have you heard talking about a great idea that they've had, but they've never bothered to do anything with it?' That sounded very familiar. I nodded.

'The power of dreams, Helen,' he said. 'You can have anything you wish for, if you believe in the power of dreams.'

The meeting had been grounding and Tim made a point of telephoning me for the next three days to check that I was doing okay and to encourage me to have faith in my future, however uncertain it may be. He had an air of tranquillity about him that gave rise to my suspicion that he must surely know something that the rest of us don't. To my amazement and Tim's unquestionable credit, I was very soon able to negotiate the rows of organic beans and butternut squash without dissolving into tears.

I'd had the shopping bags loaded in the boot of the car and was about to drive away when I looked up and happened to notice the travel agency that I've walked past for years. Tim's voice popped into my head. I stopped the engine and decided to take my positive action for the day.

'What kind of thing are you looking for?' said the loud chirpy girl with the scary highlights. She tipped her head to one side and chewed noisily on her gum while she waited for me to reach her position.

I had been hoping to get the other lady who was sitting at the next desk, but she was still busy with her frustrated baby-laden customer when Scary's position became free, so there really was no avoiding her.

'I'm not sure, really,' I said as I sat in the seat opposite her. 'I've looked through some brochures and I think I'd like to go somewhere nice and relaxing.'

'How many people is it for?' she asked in all seriousness, preparing her computer with a few confident clicks of her mouse.

'Just me,' I said.

'Oh!' she said, and stared at me in the kind of way that someone who had held the job for longer, like the lady at the next desk, wouldn't have done.

'One traveller,' she murmured slowly as she

tapped it into her computer with the flats of her fingerpads, defying the obstacles presented by her diabolic acrylic nails.

'And . . . when are you thinking of travelling?' She checked off the next question confidently and looked back at me with eyes encircled by thick hairy spider legs. I wondered how long it took her to get that many coats of mascara on. Maybe she just split the side of the tube open and blinked her lashes into it.

'I'd like to get away quite soon,' I said. 'Maybe in the next few weeks?'

'In, the, next, few, weeks,' she confirmed, keying a few more facts onto her screen.

'And . . . what's your budget?' She smiled. The 'and' was always very long and followed by a pause before the next question.

'Well I can be a bit flexible with that,' I said, not wanting to give the impression that I was either a cheapskate or a squanderer. 'In fact, I was hoping that you might have something last minute somewhere nice? Maybe you've got a good deal going somewhere exotic? You know, palm trees and white beaches. That kind of thing.'

'Mmm,' she said, staring at the screen. 'Exotic.'

She spent the next fifteen minutes or so trawling incompetently through the millions of holidays lodged irretrievably in her computer and starting to describe various destinations before saying, 'Oh sorry. That one's not available,' and then resuming her infuriatingly futile search. Just as I was about to make my excuses and head out of there, the entrance door opened and in came a tall, lanky man wearing the same staff badge as Scary. He walked towards the back of the shop, sandwich bag in hand, newspaper under his arm. As he reached his desk, which was the last one on the row of five, Scary suddenly noticed that he was back. She abandoned her computer and straightened herself towards him.

'Oi, Pete!' she called loudly. 'This lady wants to go somewhere exotic on her own as soon as possible.' Silence befell the entire travel agency and everyone stopped and peered at me knowingly. 'Got any ideas?' she added.

The man called Pete looked at me and made a snap appraisal of the situation. He then put his sandwich bag and newspaper down on his desk, sat on the edge of it and thought for a minute, gazing upwards with a furrowed brow and saying, 'Mmm,' every now and then. We all waited with baited breath for his Eureka moment. He stood up, leaped to the display and pulled down a distinctly exotic-looking long-haul brochure.

'How about India?'

CHAPTER 9

DEATH BY YOGA

I have no doubt that it was almost certainly the shocking sight of my reflection trying to arrange itself nicely into a jungle-print swimsuit that sent me scuttling off to the local leisure centre. The lady in the lingerie department had kindly offered to go and get me another size so that I didn't have to leave the safety of the changing cubicle, but as far as I could see, size was not really the issue. It was the flab factor.

Don't get me wrong. It's not as though I looked like the back end of a bus or anything. Just so long as I kept my clothes on. Fortified with an armful of vaccinations against all manner of hideous-sounding deaths, it was now just a couple of weeks before I had to bare all under a tropical sky, and I was determined not to let the side down by being not only recently widowed but pitifully out of shape. Other guests at the hotel would give me furtive glances and comment to each other that I really shouldn't be wearing a bikini with a body like that. Then they would be told quietly by one of the bar staff that I was a recently bereaved widow, and they would all feel terribly sorry for me and I would be excused persecution for my poolside crime and issued with extra peanut rations when I ordered a drink.

Besides, if those forty-somethings in the weekly gossip magazines can manage to hold their guts together in the face of their fast approaching middle age, surely a thirty-something like me could do the same with knobs on. Or maybe they all wear concrete corsets. That's why their smiles look so painful. And that strangely inhuman sideways lounging pose that so many of them adopt while showing off their borrowed evening-wear outfits, what's that all about, then?

The parable of the changing-room humiliation was clear. My foolish assumption that doing the housework religiously every day and constantly going up and down the stairs would be enough to keep me in shape had been severely misguided. With my latest lesson in positive action still ringing loudly in my ears from my last session with Tim, I took the bull by the horns and decided to join the gym generation.

'I'd like to enquire about using the gym facilities,' I said in my most toned voice to the navy-blue tracksuit on reception. He turned round. Surely he couldn't have been more than fifteen? I must be getting old.

'Okay,' he said, looking at me a little unsurely. 'Have you ever used a gym before?'

Oh God. Was it really that obvious? This was a real confidence booster.

'No,' I said, 'but I'm keen to get my fitness levels up.' For a moment I was tempted to jog on the spot a little to demonstrate my significant distance from the cemetery, but then I thought the better of it.

'Okay,' he said again, brightly this time, and he took a leaflet out of the display by the till and spread it open on the counter in front of me.

'You'll need to have a fitness assessment and an induction session before you can come along and use the gym on your own,' he explained. 'We do those on a Saturday morning at eleven o'clock.'

He circled the appropriate time on the leaflet's schedule with a biro and I went away feeling the after-glow of a perfectly acceptable workout.

What the schedule didn't say was that the tour would be attended by a small group of equally pathetic people, and when I arrived on the Saturday morning, my first reaction was to turn on my heels and run. One woman was so enormous that she looked as if she might pass out just trying to get up the stairs to check out the changing facilities. She had to keep stopping and hanging on to the rail. Maybe she had wandered in by accident thinking this was a huge, glowing bistro.

Then there was the superfit couple who, I am sure, had just come along for the entertainment factor as they flexed their supple bodies at every stopping opportunity. I dawdled and shuffled my way to the back of the group, rapidly losing interest as the tour guide explained the differing benefits of the terrifyingly complicated-looking fitness machines. The sight of the packed gymnasium filled with a variety of shapes and sizes, some puffing and panting as they urged themselves towards Heartbreak Hill in their own personal marathon, others barely breaking into a sweat as they made mincemeat of a Nautilus machine while elegantly sipping from a bottle of sporty water, horrified me.

This was definitely not for me, so I hid at the next corner and let the group continue without me before making my way back towards the entrance.

'Chickening out?' The teenage tracksuit smiled as he saw me heading off.

Cheeky little sod, I thought. It's all right for you, with your unused body and your boundless energy.

'It's not really my thing.' I wrinkled my nose and brushed the comment off as I reached for my car keys.

'Well you don't have to use the gym to get fit, you know!' he said. 'There're loads of things you can do.'

And with a crusading enthusiasm he came out from behind the reception area and selected a couple of other leaflets from the same counter-top display.

'How about doing a class?' he said. 'We've got quite a few ladies-only groups and they're very popular with the older women.'

Thwack, the sound of another nail being hammered into my coffin. I thought he was going to hand the leaflets over and so hung on there for a moment, but he just held on to them and waited for me to enthuse. Perhaps I should just punch him really hard on the nose and be done with it.

'Right,' I said.

'You don't have to do an induction or anything for the classes,' he added thoughtfully. 'And with some of them you can even just turn up in comfortable clothes and not bother with the changing rooms!' This was going from bad to worse.

'Great,' I said.

'How about yoga?' he suggested helpfully. 'Our yoga teacher's a right loon and her class is always full of ladies like you.' I wondered whether this young man's mother was proud of him.

'Steve!' The tour guide reappeared, having either lost her sheep or consigned them to the master of the torture chamber upstairs. She approached me looking all fit and fresh. Maybe I should punch her too.

'I think what Steve means is that we have a great yoga teacher here and her class is really good fun. I go myself whenever I can. It's ladies only and everyone is really, really nice.' She looked at me with a big friendly smile. 'I think you'd enjoy it!'

I was still standing there, so I guess that meant I was still interested.

'Why don't I book you in for tomorrow's session?' she asked. 'It's the Sunday afternoon slot so it's usually nice and relaxed. Not too many people.'

'Sounds good,' I said, and young Steve looked very happy indeed. He's not such a bad lad after all, I thought to myself.

Yoga. Also known as 'how to totally humiliate yourself in front of a group of complete strangers'. Why we insist on doing things like that in preparation for a two-week holiday I shall never know. That driving urge to change the habits of a lifetime for a few days so that we can pretend to be someone we're not with a lifestyle that we don't have.

I have never felt so completely ridiculous in my life. I couldn't manage even the most rudimentary of movements, my shamefully dilapidated body creaking and juddering a thundering 'no way' at even the gentlest of requests for just a couple of inches of flexibility. I was utterly appalled.

I remember vividly the nights I would go out with friends, hanging out and having a good time, dancing for hours in night clubs filled with shady-looking people, not even leaving the flat until the witching hour and then staying out until four or five in the morning. And after blasting the night away, still managing to get to my desk without fail the next morning, apart from the time I accidentally woke up in another country, but that's a different story.

Now I stared down miserably at the toes I could

no longer reach, my back welded into an agonizing sciatic spasm, my bones letting out alarmingly geriatric groans and crackling awfully, and I was still a good ten inches away from target.

As I looked down at my feet, I felt as though the distance might as well be a couple of miles, and I suddenly wished that I hadn't painted my toenails quite such a vibrant shade of pink. Julia had thought it was just the colour to complement a tropical beach holiday so I had tried it out the night before. Now as I gazed down at The Untouchables I saw only too clearly that a couple of carefully applied coats of fuchsia nail polish does not an attractive woman make. I had been spending time painstakingly painting my toes while completely neglecting the body that lived on top of them.

I tried much harder to reach, letting out a small roar of determination, and vowed to correct the error of my ways. At the end of the session, I scraped myself off the rubber mat (everyone else seemed to have brought their own far more elegant affairs) and started towards the door in a casual manner which I thought hid the intense pain rather well.

'You all right?' said the teacher brightly as she bounced to my side. 'I haven't seen you here before!'

'No,' I said, trying to keep the grimace from my face. 'This is my first time.'

'What, first time here or first time yoga?' she asked.

'First time everything,' I said.

'Well, jolly good! But I think you were pushing yourself a bit hard there.' She wagged her finger at me in a schoolmarmish way. 'Don't want you dying on me after your first class!' and she bounced towards the door and out of sight. Well that was encouraging.

'What on earth have you been doing?' asked Sara as I approached the table she had booked for us all for lunch. 'You look like you've been run over!'

'Thank you,' I said. 'And the answer to your question is yoga.'

'Yoga?!' the three of them repeated.

'Yes,' I said defiantly. 'Tim recommended that I take up some form of regular exercise to help keep me balanced and to raise my energy levels.'

'Who's Tim?' asked Leoni mischievously.

Before I could answer her question, I felt a sharp kick in my side of my leg. It could only have come from Julia, but her deadpan expression and the slight reddening of her cheeks was enough to fill in the finer details of her pain-inducing silent sentence.

'Just some bloke at the local leisure centre,' I replied casually.

'Oh yes?' she teased, and Sara started fluttering her eyelashes above the menu page and softly singing something about Tim and Helen up a tree. Well it made a change from now well-worn jokes about Dudley and His Chopper.

'Oh stop it, Sara,' I said, but we all laughed anyway and I have to say that the five yoga sessions I had survived over the last ten days really had made all the difference. Perhaps not in the bikini stakes, but certainly to my general sense of well-being, not to mention the jeans that I had finally managed to fasten without first having to lie on the bed and thrash around like a frenzied shark.

The waiter came to take our order.

'Good afternoon, ladies,' he said in a thick Italian accent. 'And how are we all today?' He took Julia's hand and kissed it serenely.

'Very well thank you, Mario,' she said graciously.

'*Bene*,' he said. 'You all know about today's specials?' he asked, nodding at each of us.

'Mario, darling, they haven't changed for fifteen years, so I think we're all familiar with them by now,' said Julia sweetly.

'I'm hurt.' Mario placed his hand on his heart and give us a look of mock sorrow. 'You want to know about my salami?' he said discreetly.

We looked at each other. Leoni blushed and seemed genuinely scared.

'Yes!' he cried. 'I have the very big salami,' and he gazed up at the ceiling, smiling enigmatically at the impressive array of charcuterie hanging from the beams.

'So I've been told, Mario,' responded Julia playfully without looking up from her menu. 'But I hear it can give a girl awful indigestion at lunchtime.'

157

Mario roared with laughter. 'I bring you some drinks,' he announced and shouted the order through to the bar in a barrage of paternal Italiano.

We lunched on the most delicious banquet of sea creatures and salad, the conversation meandering between pointless topics as the bread was passed round, everyone comfortable and happy, and it felt like old times. I had to pinch myself once or twice, and I felt enormously blessed that I was back here once more.

'Nice ring,' commented Sara as she sought to release a poor unsuspecting mollusc fighting a futile battle to stay attached to its once safe and secure home.

I had picked it up the day before from the jeweller, who offered me next to nothing for my wedding and engagement rings. I accepted the laughable payment without emotion, having no further use for the tokens that had bought my years of dedication so cheaply. My new mistress-intended bauble was going to serve as a spangling reminder for me to think twice before trusting another man.

'It's the one you found in Robert's desk,' I said, looking at it again. 'I had it altered.'

'Pudding?' said Leoni enthusiastically, changing the subject.

'Well I used to be,' I said. 'But I'm a lot slimmer now.'

'So, Helen,' said Sara. 'when are you going to drag yourself into the twenty-first century and get yourself an email address?'

'Email? No thank you,' I said.

I had recently switched to Waitrose now that my grocery budget was well and truly my own, and I had got myself into the most dreadful pickle with the scan-it-yourself contraption. By the time I reached the checkout with my meagre basket of provisions, I had somehow managed to rack up a grand total approaching two hundred pounds. The staff were at a complete loss to understand how one person could make such a prize-winning hash of their idiot-proof system, and I happily went back to the age-old tradition of queuing up instead. Tim had encouraged me to embrace every new experience that came my way and to try out as many new things as I could. This, my first foray into modern technology, had proved my point all along. Helen, plus anything technological, equals unmitigated disaster.

'Even I've got email!' said Leoni proudly, swinging her shoulders from side to side and closing her eyes. 'So it must be easy! God, remember that week when I got that so-called intelligent washing machine?'

'How could I forget,' quipped Julia.

'No?' I said.

I had missed just about everything interesting during my years of enforced confinement, but it made for great conversation as everyone rolled out their favourite you'll-never-guess-what-happened stories.

'What happened?' I asked.

159

'She electrocuted herself,' said Julia.

'My God!' I said, horrified. 'Were you okay?'

'Yes!' laughed Leoni. 'The power surge gave my brain such a jolt that I felt brilliant for about a week! It was a proper electric shock with hair sticking out and everything! Marcus had to prise me off with a broom handle!'

'You are kidding me!' I said. Her triumphant look assured me that she was not, and she cracked the top of her crème brûlée with a confident smack of her spoon.

'I'll teach you how to use it,' offered Sara.

Oh dear. We were back on the email trail again. I thought I'd managed to bat that one nicely out of the field. I tried to look interested although I would far rather have heard more about Leoni putting all the lights out down their street.

'It's not all it's cracked up to be,' Julia grumbled, 'although I suppose it would be if someone could come up with an answer to the world spam crisis.'

'That's unwanted emails, isn't it?' I said knowledgeably, doing my best not to sound as though I had been living in a cave for the last decade.

'Millions of them,' said Julia.

Leoni nodded her head in agreement.

'Most of mine seem to be from people advertising sexual gratification. I had one this morning offering to come over if I was feeling lonely. That was nice.' Leoni's eyes glazed over as she indulged her senses in the X-rated erotica of her creamy

160

dessert. 'Then there are those flagrant promises of a larger penis or a better quality erection,' she said. 'They're jolly tempting but Marcus has insisted that I have to make do with his.'

'Boo, spoilsport,' said Sara.

'And it's great for drugs,' added Leoni taking a large swig of wine. 'The Valium's come in very handy and I don't have to run the gauntlet of Dr Snootypants at the surgery any more. But I've not managed to find Ritalin anywhere. Can't get it on the black market for love nor money.'

'Leoni!' Sara gasped. 'You haven't! They could be sending you any old thing!'

'I bloody well have,' she said. 'And my family should thank their lucky stars that I ordered Valium instead of hemlock. You can get it quite easily, you know.'

'And mushrooms,' added Julia.

We looked to her for more information.

'There are these mushrooms you can get which are deadly poisonous,' she whispered. 'Apparently they don't have a strong taste and the poison in them disperses very quickly and is completely undetectable at post-mortem stage.'

'Really?' gushed Leoni. 'Well I never. What are they called?'

'Christ, I don't know!' responded Julia to the disappointed Leoni before turning to me. 'It's a really handy way to keep in touch when you're away.'

'I'll think about it,' I said. 'I expect I'll get around to it at some point.'

Mario brought the coffees and Leoni searched in her handbag before pulling out a bottle of Rescue Remedy. She unscrewed the top and poured the entire contents into her coffee cup and gave it a delicate stir.

'How's Marcus?' I asked her.

'Fine,' she said flatly. 'Dropping huge hints all over the place that he's not getting enough sex. And it's so transparent.'

We leaned forwards into the table. Leoni looked as though she was about to dish it.

'He starts off by taking a long shower and whistling like a bus conductor. Then he has a really obvious and noisy shave, and then he sits within my view trimming and smoothing his nails.' We all start sniggering. 'And then he starts with the big yawning and stretching routine at ten o'clock and brings "early night" and "feeling a bit tired" into the conversation even though I'm engrossed in a film and he's not actually talking to anyone at all.'

'What do you do?' Sara asked, her face shining with amusement.

'Well you can't put it off forever, can you? So I usually give in but it's all so bloody predictable. You know, you get to the bedroom and there he is, lying in bed with his hands behind his head, stinking of cologne and waiting for something to happen. So I just let him get on with it and think about the shopping.'

We were all laughing by then.

'I've been getting my period twice a month.' She winked. 'It's a total nightmare this pre-menopause syndrome, isn't it?'

Nice one, Leoni.

As I finished the packing and tried hopelessly to persuade the case to close under the strain of my incompetent attempt at travellin' light, I could hardly contain the building sense of excitement that welled up inside me. The ticket jumped up and down on the dressing table singing 'Tropical Heatwave' and joshing noisily with the passport next to it, and I felt wickedly irresponsible for having upgraded myself to the comfort of the premium-class cabin for the imminent long-haul flight.

An hour or so later, I tidied my hair in the reflection of the little bull's-eye glass window set into Carol's front door and hoped that the armful of pink peonies that I had bought at the florist's would not appear too ostentatious. I hadn't meant to be excessive, it was just that they all looked so happy together in the bucket that I couldn't bring myself to separate them from their siblings.

'Oh my goodness!' exclaimed Carol as she opened her door. 'I do hope those aren't for me!'

'I'm afraid so,' I apologized.

Carol swept up the huge bunch of gargantuan flowers into her hands and laughed out loud.

'They're magnificent!' she exclaimed. 'I can't grow these in my garden! Goodness knows I've tried, but they just won't have it. Come in!' she waved. 'I'll just get these into some water before they start gasping.'

I followed her into her kitchen.

'Coffee? Tea?' she said as she filled an enormous vase under the tap.

'I'd love to, Carol, but I really can't stay. I'm off on holiday tomorrow morning and I wondered if I could ask you to keep an eye on the house for me while I'm away?'

'Holiday?' she said, looking over her shoulder at me from the sink. 'How lovely! Going anywhere nice?' She returned to the flowers.

Why do we always say that when we hear that someone is going on holiday? Well I was hardly likely to be going somewhere horrible, was I? I can see it now: come to sunny Baghdad and forget about all your troubles at home.

'I haven't decided yet,' I lied.

I just didn't particularly feel like talking, and the pictures in my head were so much better than anything I could have said out loud.

'So I'm taking myself and my suitcase to the airport and we're going for international cupboard surprise.' Blimey, that was good, I thought.

'Gosh, that's very brave of you,' said Carol, looking deeply impressed. 'I'd like to do that myself one day. You know –' she waved her hand in the air as she fantasized '– just take off and see where the breeze takes me.'

164

It would have to be a bloody strong breeze, Carol.

I held up the key that I had taken with me and put it down on the worktop. She picked it up and dropped it in her apron pocket and squeezed my arm in a neighbourly way.

'No trouble at all,' she said. 'You just go and enjoy yourself.'

I went home and took a long, hot bath, filled right up to my chin in a baptism of wonderful-smelling oils. Then I retreated to the comfort of my bedroom where I had decided to spend the rest of the evening creating the perfect pre-holiday skin.

While I waited for multiple regions to dry, I settled myself in front of the television with a nice cup of tea and watched the primped but persecuted woman on the spousal-exchange programme clearing up some other ghastly family's dog turds from their Steptoe and Son back yard. It then switched to a picture of an allegedly female slob lying around on wife number one's luxurious velour sofa, watching a slanging match on daytime television, chain-smoking cheap cigarettes and dropping her ash all over the cream carpet. Cut back to the Sloane in Dog Shit City.

She has got to be completely out of her mind, I thought to myself as the bottom of my over-dunked biscuit fell into the cup with a plop.

★   ★   ★

I woke up way before the alarm sounded reveille, but forced myself to stay put in bed with my eyes closed in the hope that I wouldn't peak too early on such a red-letter day – like a small child becoming so overexcited at the prospect of their birthday party in the afternoon that they exhaust themselves completely and end up sleeping through the whole thing. I reasoned with myself that if I stayed absolutely still and kept my eyes gently closed it wasn't too far removed from the feat of actually being asleep, so surely I would wake up a bag-free zone.

Sixty minutes later, as I reached the bathroom yawningly and greeted my reflection in the mirror, it became wildly apparent that the odd bag here or there would have been the least of my worries. After a triple take, there was no mistaking this particular morning glory.

I was orange.

I stopped dead in my tracks and tried to take in the full wide-screen cinemascope version of the horror movie staring back at me. My hand flew to my open mouth. I rushed closer to the mirror and looked again with my face just inches away.

'Holy shit! What have I done?' came the plaintive cry in my head. I turned on more lights. I desperately reached for a flannel and rinsed it under the tap before trying hopelessly to rub off the tangerine mask. Then I remembered. I stood back and lifted my nightie and there, in all its glory, was my orange body. Only this time, we had stripes too. Nice.

Twenty minutes of vicious scrubbing in a meltingly hot shower served only to turn me into a red-raw effigy of a post-radiation-leak victim who had been hosed down with acid. I was so hot I thought I was going to faint. Look, just calm down, I told myself. Sit down, for God's sake, and have a cup of tea or something. There's absolutely nothing you can do about it so you might as well just stop panicking and get your head around it.

I don't know whose idea the make-up was. Mine, I expect. By the time the taxi arrived and started bibbing impatiently from the road I had managed to create the perfect panto-mime dame. I rushed outside, doing my best to hide the damage behind a big dressing gown with the hood pulled up around my offensive burned-marmalade head.

'Excuse me.' I tapped on the window.

The bored-looking driver tore his eyes away from his super sensational soar-away *Sun*.

'I'm running a bit late and I'll be about ten minutes,' I said. 'Will you just hang on there, please?'

'Bloody hell, love,' he said, peering closely at my face. 'You got scarlet fever or something?'

'Just wait there and I'll be back in a few minutes.' And I scurried back to the house to wash off the make-up and gather up my brain.

★　★　★

'Ticket and passport, please,' came the singsong voice from the check-in girl. She wasn't looking up, as is the habit of airport staff who are trained not to make eye contact with their passengers. I noticed critically that she had slipped up by saying 'please'.

'Put your luggage on the belt, please.' She examined the ticket and tapped a few things into her computer to start the baggage stickers spewing out of the ugly little machine next to her.

'Did you pack these bags yourself?'

'Yes,' I said.

'Do you have any of these items in your hand luggage?' She placed a laminated sheet on the counter and tapped it with her pen. On it were listed various items in words and then in pictures for the hard of hearing. Scissors, butane-powered curling tongs, guns, that kind of thing.

'No,' I said.

'Your flight will be boarding from gate twenty-one at about quarter to three.'

She handed me back my ticket and, sackable offence, she looked at me.

I've never had anyone stare at me quite like that before. She was completely lost for words. She frowned a little and looked closer. I looked back at her without expression. That's the thing about having something bizarre literally written across your face. You can't see it. You don't feel any different inside, like you would if you had, say, leprosy or something, so you don't think you look any different on the outside, and I had for a few merciful minutes forgotten that I had been Tangoed.

Her lip curled a little, but she tried not to look disgusted or too alarmed.

'Madam, are you fit to travel?'

'I beg your pardon?' I said indignantly.

'You look like you have a serious condition,' she said, this time taking on a slightly more official tone with me and preparing herself to spring into action with the guidelines set out on page sixteen of the training manual about how to deal with deadly tropical diseases at the check-in desk.

I leaned towards her.

'It's a self-tanning disaster,' I whispered to her discreetly as the sighs and tuts from the waiting passengers elevated to an 'Oh for God's sake will you move along there' from a grumpy old man towards the back end of the queue.

'Crikey,' she said. 'What did you use?'

'Self-tan,' I said, just managing to stop myself from adding 'stupid' to the end of the sentence.

'No, I mean what make?' she said. 'I wouldn't want to accidentally go and use the same stuff myself, would I?'

CHAPTER 10

ENLIGHTEN ME

Simoné had been an absolute godsend and had seemed uncontrollably excited at the prospect of helping me to create his take on the perfect holiday capsule wardrobe. As I stepped off the plane into the searing heat of a true Indian summer, I was glad of the cooling effects of the loose-fitting white linen tunic and trousers – part linen pyjama edging towards shalwar kameez – that he had insisted were the perfect travelling companions. I did look every inch the seasoned traveller, if still a little orange despite the fake-tan remover I had found in the airport branch of Boots. After humouring me for the first half hour, Simoné had gently but firmly steered me away from my predictable choices of colourful strappy dresses and little tops, explaining that as a woman travelling alone in such a heady climate, I might feel more comfortable if I were dressed in something a little 'less trashy'. Like a no-nonsense doctor, when it comes to fashion Simoné gives it to you straight.

We were herded from the aeroplane into a chaotic rigmarole of check-points and officials, each one of them bearing a different rubber stamp or coloured slip of paper which had to be displayed or kept safe ready to hand in at the next barrier. To lose any one of these talismans would no doubt incur the penalty of going immediately to jail without passing Go. After the long flight, I had engaged my personal autopilot in an attempt to safely navigate my discombobulated way through the uncharted territory of a part-time minor Indian airport.

The formality of all the officials' dress, despite the oppressive heat, made me grateful that I had abandoned the usual holiday-flight ensemble, and I noticed that the women who had opted for the kind of thing that I might normally have worn were receiving disapproving glances from the ladies manning passport control.

'Bags, madam! Bags, madam!' insisted the brown-shirted porter who had appeared in front of me as I emerged into the arrivals pen and was now trying to wrestle the luggage trolley from my hands. There were dozens of them teeming towards us from every direction, all dressed in the same uniform and vying for the attentions of the new influx of passengers. Fantastic, I thought. I watched a man arguing hotly with one and telling him to get off. How ignorant. Must have been travelling in the economy cabin. Probably not used to having people waiting on him.

I wish the service was like this in the European holiday resort airports, instead of having to deal with the usual bun fight as the entire passenger list of the midday charter flight from Stansted starts fighting over just twelve trolleys all chained together in the far corner of baggage reclaim. There's always one smarty-pants with a correct local currency coin at the ready who then makes away smugly with his prize.

Yes, this was far more civilized.

I gladly let the porter take my trolley and he showed me a one-pound coin. I looked at it and he said something I couldn't understand then pointed at me, pointed at the coin, and pointed at himself.

'Oh right!' I said, and I fished a pound coin from the side pocket of my bag and gave it to him.

With that, he promptly took off at a rate of knots, so I went after him and tried to keep my wits about me. Didn't want to be getting lost in the airport five minutes after touchdown, now did we? It took him all of ten seconds to reach the terminal doors, where he promptly abandoned my trolley amid the chaos outside then disappeared back into the arrivals hall. By the time I turned around to shout 'Oi!' he was gone.

I took hold of the trolley and tried to get my bearings, squinting painfully against the bright sun, scanning the unfamiliar surroundings and wondering which particular thronging crowd would be my best bet for some onward assistance. Another porter appeared.

'Bags, madam!' he said as he tried to grapple the trolley away from me.

'Get off!' I snapped, and possessively wrenched the handle back.

As I tried to negotiate my way through each frenetic crowd pocket, I began to wonder if I had not perhaps been a little ambitious with my destination, then, like a sign from the heavens, I saw a man loitering around holding a piece of paper with my name written on it in big letters. At least, I think it was my name. Miss Rubbins, it said. I put my hand up high, waving frantically in his direction, the way you would if you were desperate to show off to the teacher that you knew the answer. He noticed my overenthusiastic 'pick me' identity tag and waved back at me.

'Hello!' I said.

'Yes, certainly,' he said, and he helped the bags into the trunk of the battle-scarred little round yellow car while I settled myself onto the back seat. He had religious paraphernalia and godly artefacts arranged all over the dashboard, with two rosaries swinging from the rear-view mirror and a picture of Jesus looking very holy stuck to the front of the glove compartment.

The taxi pulled away from the airport, and as the little car struggled over several axle-splitting craters, Jesus went from head up and hands apart in open blessing, to head down and palms clasped together in dignified prayer. Five minutes and several near misses later, it became abundantly clear why all the vehicles were adorned in this way. Bumper stickers with slogans like 'Jesus Save Me' and excerpts from the Last Rites flashed in front of me as the driver slammed his foot on the accelerator, pulling out into the path of oncoming trucks and jay-walking holy cows before screeching to a halt and pulling back in just seconds before certain impact.

I held on to both door handles and anchored my feet at either side of the rise in the middle of the floral-carpeted floor and tried to go with the jangling music blaring from the radio. In the corner of my eye I thought for a moment that I could see a group of people looking in at me through the open window as we were careering along. My sideways glance was met with the memorable picture of five young men crammed precariously onto an old motorbike. The driver noticed my dismay at the sight of the amateur display team.

'They get fined if they are caught,' he shouted, looking over his shoulder at me and pointing his thumb out of the window at the overloaded bike.

We drove deeper and deeper into the lush vegetation, leaving the bedlam of the city behind as the overcrowded buses and painted trucks gradually gave way to a slightly gentler pace of mopeds, bicycles and a handful of mainly ancient cars. I looked out of the window at the different world passing me by. The dusty red-dirt road was shaded by age-old coconut palms flanking each side, rising high into the hazy pink sky, with the way punctuated here and there by roughly assembled shacks and stalls selling fresh produce and live chickens from wooden cages. We waited at an invisible junction for no apparent reason, and I noticed a little off-white structure, rather like an emergency outside dunny, with a home-made sign daubed on cardboard propped up against the door. Starbucks Internet Cafe, it said. I'd like to see Starbucks try to sue that.

I felt the car take a sharp right and head towards the ocean, but before my eyes could follow the new direction, a bone-jarring crash brought the car to an immediate and unceremonious halt. My head rattled badly and for a moment I couldn't see a thing as I tried to compose myself and fought to restore my blurred vision. The music from the radio seemed to increase to an unbearable volume. I looked down and saw that I was covered in shards of glass. One glance in the direction of the driver confirmed my suspicion that we had lost this particular heat of chicken run.

Both drivers were out of their vehicles, in the other man's case a truck that had come from out of nowhere, laden with vegetables, and they were shouting at each other and waving their hands around. A few people gathered to watch, standing about casually and fanning themselves now and again, and the traffic, both wheeled and legged, started to back up on both sides. I got out of the car and tried to shake the fragments of broken window from my clothes, pinching the fabric of my tunic and holding it away from myself as I waggled around. Now both the drivers were just hanging out with the rest of the crowd.

'Excuse me,' I said, not wanting to appear rude. No one seemed to notice my presence.

'Excuse me!' I shouted. 'Do you think we could get going or do we have to call the police?' They looked rather surprised, finished their conversation and the driver came back to the car.

'Yes we get going now, madam,' he said, and he put a blanket over the back seat to cover up any small remnants of glass that might have been missed.

We pulled away, weaving our way through the carnage we had created, and returned to the middle of the road. The driver put his foot down again as though nothing had happened and Jesus frantically switched between blessing and praying as the little car bravely soldiered on towards its next catastrophe.

Pulling open the curtains, I was consoled the following morning by the sight of tall white egrets picking their way elegantly through the grass as the sprinklers threw their morning rations to the straining shiny leaves of the tropical plants in the exquisite gardens outside my palatial room. I had upgraded that too. And the hotel.

Breakfast was the most thrilling affair. I was shown to a film-location table on the open-air terrace with panoramic views across the gardens to the sparkling Arabian Sea beyond. Three smart waiters attended to my every need, the first one moving the chair out for me and holding the back in readiness to bring it in to the table, the second standing by with a starched napkin ready to place into my lap, the third with a white linen cloth folded neatly over his forearm, overseeing that everything was done impeccably, and waiting to hear my preference for tea or coffee. A small glass of chilled, fresh mango juice was presented to me on a silver salver, and was soon followed by a delicious breakfast of perfectly poached eggs, a little bacon, toast and warm croissants with mouth-wateringly fruity jams. At last, I was sitting pretty in the very lap of luxury.

Join us for yoga in the garden. Every morning at 8 invited the sign in the lobby. I made a mental note and headed for the pool. It was every bit as luxurious as the breakfast, and one of the nice pool attendants created for me a personal enclave complete with steamer chair, a small table, and a vast parasol.

I relaxed into my lounger and tried to get into my new book. It was the big bestseller that everyone was reading at the moment, so I thought I might as well have a go at updating my popular culture, although I have to say that from the description on the back it was not really my thing. But, I had reasoned, never judge a book by its cover.

An hour or so later I realized that I was just staring at the words on the page, and I didn't have the faintest idea what was going on, or who this character with the knife was, or why he was about to kill the Chinese chef with the missing tooth. I put the book down and looked around. The pool area had filled up a little more now. I watched some children playing with a ball in the water while an old lady diligently swam length after length as best she could in the freeform space, moving with the steady pace of a migrating whale.

As she came up for a breath, the ball hit her square in the face. She spluttered and stood up, pulling the goggles from her eyes and violently coughing up the water from her lungs. Recovering herself sufficiently to give them a good earful, she shouted angrily in Russian and shook her fist at the children who were desperately trying to rescue their ball before she bit it in half. The woman's husband appeared by the steps, and they started shouting at each other angrily and tried to get the pool attendants to organize a public hanging. One of the attendants walked off and the other just shrugged his shoulders and pointed at the children by way of an explanation. The Russians shook their heads in a critical damnation of the regime's reluctance to crush the insurgents.

'Are you English?' asked the slight, bespectacled woman who had mysteriously appeared at my side.

'Yes,' I said, just a split second before realizing that I should have said '*Nyet*'.

'Ooh. We thought so! I saw you at breakfast and I said to my daughter, "You know, I bet she's English."'

I smiled at her politely.

'Are you here on your own?' she persisted. 'It's just that I noticed you've only got one lounger set up so I thought to myself, you know, I bet she's on her own!'

'Well spotted.' No shit, Sherlock.

'Husband didn't want to come, I expect,' she said knowingly with a little frown and shake of her head. 'Mine neither. He does it every time.' She gave an exasperated sigh. 'So here we are again, just me and Katie, that's my daughter, you know,' she filled me in. 'So I thought, right, you bastard, and I booked the most expensive holiday I could find.' She gave me a satisfied nod. 'Well he did say to me, "Just go and book what you want but for Pete's sake stop nagging me, woman." So I did!'

My smile changed from polite to highly amused.

'I intercepted his post for the next few weeks and tore up his credit card statement so that he wouldn't find out and make me cancel it. Thinks we're in Spain! Should be finding out anytime around . . .' she looked at her watch, 'now. My name's Meg,' she said.

'Helen,' I replied. 'And I don't have a husband any more. He's dead.'

'Oh my goodness, I am so sorry! Oh what an idiot!' Her face flushed and she looked completely mortified.

'Don't be,' I said. 'It sounds like we were married to the same man.'

★   ★   ★

Santash, the Ayurvedic doctor, took numerous pulses as he watched my face intently, pushing hard into tender points under my eyes and all over the place, and suddenly I felt as though I had been exposed. My curiosity visit had somehow turned into a full-blown consultation with one of the three doctors, and he took detailed notes of his findings and discussed his new patient with one of his colleagues before delivering his verdict.

'You are not sleeping at night?' I wasn't expecting the question.

'Well I wouldn't say that I'm not sleeping . . .' I began.

'Yes, but you are waking up how many times? Four? Five?'

'About that,' I said. I hadn't been paying too much attention to my sleep patterns since everything changed. I thought it was probably due to all the upset recently, but the tiresome ritual of waking up and then trying to get back to sleep had definitely started to take its toll. Hence the holiday.

Santash sat back in his chair and held his pen pointedly.

'You are suffering from complete mental exhaustion,' he said matter of factly.

I was shocked, but not surprised. The shock had been the caring and gentle manner in which this man had said virtually nothing as he examined my eyes and skin and moved around my joints taking note of the pulses in each place. His intermittent questions had been very specific, and had seemed more a case of him confirming his own thoughts. It was all a far cry from the three-minute in and out at my local health centre. Now, having arrived at his diagnosis, he watched me intently as I took it on board, as though waiting for the reaction he had already predicted.

I felt my nostrils flare a little, the way that they do when I'm trying not to get emotional and determined to hold back any rogue tears. I nodded.

'How long are you staying here for?' he asked.

'Two weeks,' I replied.

'Good,' he said. 'We need you here every day and you will have an intense programme of treatment.' Santash began writing out the prescription, which ran to two pages, before explaining it to me as he pointed to each part of the schedule.

'You will be woken at seven with herbal remedy, like tea,' he explained. 'You can put honey in it if you want to. So you drink that then you come to the garden by the viewing point for eight o'clock where you will do yoga and meditation. You know the viewing point?'

'No,' I said.

'You just ask anyone and they will show you,' he said. 'Then you go to have some breakfast, something light like juice, and we see you back here at ten o'clock for rejuvenation.' I nodded. 'Then you go and do what you want in the afternoon and we see you here again at six for your evening treatment.'

I looked at the schedule then at Santash. I had been planning excursions, indeed I had a whole series of elaborate adventures in mind, involving spice plantations and bathing with elephants. Had I wanted to check myself into hospital for a fortnight I would have thrown myself under the hoofs of one of the oncoming water buffalo we had narrowly missed on the way in.

'Every day,' he repeated, as though having read my thoughts. 'It's very important for you.'

The rest of the afternoon went by in a haze as I thought about the consequences of my chance visit to the clinic. I saw Meg later by the pool and we got chatting again so I asked her about what treatments she was having.

'Oh anything!' she said. 'I'm getting rejuvenation at the moment and it's better than sex.'

'Really?' I asked. 'I'm having that tomorrow.'

'You'll love it,' said Meg as she tried to get one of the pool waiters' attention.

'So, where's your daughter?' I asked her. 'Katie, isn't it?'

'Yes. She's gone off down to the beach to get a henna tattoo done. I've told her not to let them use the black stuff. It causes terrible permanent damage. So she's having a little brown one somewhere discreet. Have you seen some of those horror stories about holiday tattoos on the telly?'

'No,' I said.

'Well.' Meg signed for the coffee she had ordered

and continued her graphic description of the pained teenager showing off the horribly scarred skin on the small of her back while the mother complained about how it shouldn't be allowed. Meg had taken up residence on the end of my lounger, forcing me to pull my knees up higher than was comfortable, and showed no sign of leaving as she sat back to enjoy her coffee.

The distinctive slouching flip-flopping steps of the bored teenager caught our attention. I couldn't see her face. It was obscured by the low-slung parasol. What I could see was the big sunburst design surrounding her pierced navel and the string of painted leaves that now served as a semi-permanent belt around her slender hips. All of it black.

Meg was horrified.

'Katie!' she shrilled. 'What did I tell you about black henna?' She was standing up now, holding Katie's arm and turning her this way and that as she stared at the enormous tattoos now adorning her daughter's body. Katie looked at me confrontationally and raised her sullen eyebrows as her mother surveyed the damage and did her pieces.

'Oh don't worry about it, Mum,' she muttered. 'God, you're so risk averse.'

And she pulled her arm out of her mother's grip and slouched off towards the bar. Meg just stood there with her hands on either side of her head.

'She's a bloody nightmare, that kid,' she said. 'Thinks she knows everything. Absolutely hates me and her father,' she added, shaking her head incredulously. 'Wants to be a bloody artist, would you believe?'

'An artist?' I said. 'That's nice.'

'Nice? It's ridiculous is what it is. We've told her, either teacher or nurse. That way, you've always got a job and you'll get a good pension.'

'Right.' I nodded. 'Very wise.'

'Mmm,' said Meg. 'Well you tell her that. She certainly won't hear it from me, or her father. Didn't do me any harm, did it?'

It turned out that Meg was a teacher, and I suspect that she was one of those teachers that you meet on parents' evening to discuss the trouble she's been having with your child, and then come home with your sympathies squarely down on the side of your kid. Her blinkers were magnificent.

The rejuvenation was unlike anything I have ever experienced. Two attendants swept, kneaded and massaged me to the very edge of consciousness. They moved in complete unison, like a perfect pas de deux in a ballet of gracefully rehearsed motions, with handfuls of hot, pungent oil so generously poured that it dripped and collected into a slippery pool on the surface of the heavy teak table that I was lying on.

That morning during the yoga and meditation session in the garden, the old and serene yogi had paid special attention to me, not allowing me to undertake some of the movements, explaining that they were not good for me, and bending my wrists and fingers with his until they let out little cracks. I had become rather emotional because he had been so nice. Here was a complete stranger showing me the sort of care and kindness that I had rarely, if ever, felt. I hadn't even realized that I craved it so.

'You come to the clinic at ten?' he asked. I found his English difficult to understand so I had to concentrate hard when he spoke.

'Yes,' I said.

My appetite had completely vanished, and when I went for breakfast I found that I really didn't want anything other than the fresh juice that Santash had suggested. After the cleansing morning of yoga and meditation, the juice tasted fresher and more delicious than it had on the previous day. I walked on the beach for a little while to contemplate the difficult thoughts still plaguing my mind, the sand underfoot giving way with little squeaks like the softest demerara, before I headed back to the clinic.

As the rejuvenation treatment began, the door opened and in came the old yogi. He leaned his face down near to mine, put his hand on the back of my head and instructed me.

'Do not think,' he said. 'Follow the movement of the hands in your mind. Do not think about anything else. Only follow the hands.'

And with that he left the room and the two hours of intensive oiling and massaging began. As I lay there and tried my best to shut out all thoughts and concentrate only on the hands that attended me, tears streamed from my eyes. I didn't feel as though I was crying. It was more like an involuntary reflex. My head began to pound, and after some time I felt as though I had been lifted out of my body and was floating in another layer outside the small, darkened chamber.

I opened my eyes. Santash was looking at me with a smile. I must have fallen asleep.

'You are finished now,' he said. 'I will leave you to dress. We don't do steam today. It will make you too weak.'

He was waiting for me in his little consulting room at the side of the clinic reception when I emerged.

'How are you feeling?' he said.

'Fine,' I said.

I didn't think it was appropriate for me to try to explain that I was actually completely spaced out and not entirely in control of my faculties.

'Drink this,' he said, and he placed in front of me a little earthenware pot filled with a couple of inches of a hot, brownish-looking viscous liquid. I picked it up and sniffed it. It smelled utterly appalling. I pulled at face at Santash.

'I said drink it! Not smell it!' He laughed. 'All in one go. Come on, it's not so bad!'

'What's in it?' I asked dubiously.

'Don't ask! Just drink it!'

I took my life in my hands and threw back the shot. My ungainly reaction upon swallowing was to clutch at my face and throat and make some very unladylike gagging noises, apologizing with the odd burst of 'God, that's disgusting' as I tried to pull myself together. Santash chuckled.

'You'll get used to it. This one is better.' And he gave me a bottle of brown watery medicine which he described as a tonic wine and told me to take four times a day. Granted, it wasn't a patch on the vileness of the other one, but still it led me to conclude that Santash was certainly no wine buff.

Noticing Meg hanging around near my lounger, I made a detour through the gardens behind the pool and headed back towards the beach. It was hot, and I hadn't brought my hat, which was still on my seat under the Rottweiler guard of Katie's mother. I did think about retrieving it, but decided that running the risk of a touch of sunstroke was preferable to the entanglement of another brain-rattling round of what Katie did next.

I slipped off my flowery sandals as the sand became firmer towards the water's edge. Tiny little sand crabs darted in and out of their homes exposed by the low tide and busied themselves rolling minuscule footballs as they sifted for their invisible nourishment. Telltale shapes on the wet shoreline gave away the location of hundreds of starfish. I bent down and carefully scraped away the top inch or so of sand, revealing the little cosmic creatures and admiring them before returning them to the surface and watching them sink their extraordinary bodies back into the planet. The sea lapped around my feet like a warm bath.

'Hello, lady!' came the friendly shout from one of the smiling women now approaching me from a little way up the beach. They all waved and I waved back. It was too hot to move, so I waited for them to reach me, the layers of their colourful saris flapping gently in the insufficient breeze as they made their way across the sand with their brightly tied bundles.

Meg had warned me about the beach sellers. Thieves, all of them. Said that she never goes onto the beach herself because you can't get a moment's peace and that something really ought to be done. She also made sure that I was fully aware of the dangers of eating at any of the beach shacks, saying that acute food poisoning, at the very least amoebic dysentery, was a certain outcome. That was a shame, I thought, as I watched a handful of people enjoying a freshly caught lunch in the shade at one of the death cafes on the sand.

'You buy something nice from me?' said the lady in the red and orange cotton sari as she stood at the edge of the water, and she motioned for me to follow her up onto the dry sand.

'I need something to cover my head,' I said as I sat down beside her. The other ladies sat around too, and they all started untying their bundles and pulling things out for me to look at.

'Not you!' said the one who had captured me, and she angrily shoved one of the other women who was putting things in front of me, and they all started arguing in heated Rajasthani. It became quite alarming, and before I knew what I was saying, I heard my King Solomon decree.

'There's no need to fight. I'll buy something from all of you.'

Anyone would have thought that I had announced a public holiday as they all started chattering excitedly, and the youngest of the ladies, who may not yet have been fourteen years old, ran off up the beach, holding the cotton of her sari above her head in a wide blue shade that billowed behind her. The remaining women spread cloths out on the sand and started setting out silver jewellery and beautifully embroidered bedspreads and cushion covers among their many splendoured things. I looked in the direction of the excited voices to see the young woman in blue heading back towards us, trailing a small army of other beach sellers, all with bundles under their arms or balanced on their heads. Clearly this was another of those impulsive decisions that I hadn't thought through properly. When would I learn?

'You very nice lady!' said one of them. 'I call you sister!' And we sat together for most of the afternoon in great comfort once Seema showed me how to create a canopy of shade with the lovely purple and green silk sarong that I paid far too much for.

Business was slow, they complained. It was late in the season and most of the tourists had gone.

After the last charter flights hauled out, these women would make their way back to their home states, where they would eek out the money they had made before returning to start the whole cycle again once the monsoons abated and the tourists reappeared. In the meantime, the hotel would be filled mainly with Indians who, they said, never bought anything from the beach sellers and treated them with contempt.

One of the ladies suddenly called out a signal like a meerkat, having spotted some other foreigners walking onto their patch. The women quickly gathered up their bundles and headed towards the figures in the heat haze, shouting 'Hello, lady!' and waving as soon as their new targets came within earshot.

I shouldered the enormous bundle of goods that I had somehow got shanghaied into buying and settled myself at a little table in one of the beach shacks, ordering a Coke from the smiling man who had been watching my spontaneous shopping spree.

'I think maybe you bought too much?' He smiled as he removed the metal top and put the cold bottle on the table.

'Yes,' I admitted shamefully.

He had the most exquisitely beautiful face with pale brown eyes and a generous mouth set into a perfect frame of high cheekbones and shiny, dark hair that rested just above his shoulders.

'You like something to eat?' he asked.

'No, thank you. The Coke is fine,' I said.

He came back to the table a while later with a little plate of fried pakoras and put them down in front of me.

'You should eat something,' he said, and he walked to the end of the shack and looked out towards the sea as he lit a cigarette. Only two of the other tables were occupied, one by a handsome middle-aged couple who treated each other tenderly, held hands and spoke quietly, and the other by a fat lady of indeterminable age with naturally white hair and real tattoos on her reddened, over-sunned skin. I relaxed and joined in with the afternoon routine of sitting around doing nothing.

When Godfrey, as I later heard him called by the white-haired trucker lady, came to see if I wanted anything else, the plate of pakoras was empty and I thanked him for bringing them.

'They were delicious,' I said.

He smiled as if he knew.

A week of intensive treatment finally broke through my well-crafted and jealously guarded surface. My mind had stopped working and my head felt like a bucket that had been filled to over-flowing and could no longer retain any information. Try as hard as I might, I couldn't find the escape valve to let any of it out, and could now barely remember what was being said to me from one moment to the next.

My digestive system had all but closed itself

down, and I found myself unable to face the thought of food and so continued to live on a little fruit, some juice and the herbal tea, and the delicious morsels that Godfrey insisted on bringing me each afternoon when I went to seek solace in the friendly tranquillity of his shack.

'Try this and tell me what you think,' he would say, before leaving me to enjoy the peace. Each day he brought me something different, always freshly prepared and delicately presented, always totally scrumptious. By the second week, he had added a blossom to the side of the plate. One humid, lazy afternoon with the shack empty, he invited me into the kitchen and showed me how to make the pakoras, encouraging me to beat the batter harder until it bubbled and making sure that I kept a safe distance from the hot fat smoking in the shallow black pan on the open stove.

After the first burst of treatment Santash had placed a hand on my shoulder and gently asked me to tell him what it was in my heart that was making me so sad. But I could not possibly say.

'You must ask me anything you want to,' Santash said.

But I did not know what to ask. So I sat there in silence and took my medicine, having learned now to hold my nose to diminish the onslaught against my namby-pamby Western palate.

'You must accept what you are.' He smiled. 'You must not think. You just have to be.'

I had been trying to get my head around that mantra for days, but it just made my brain tired and I didn't like to say that I had given up trying to chase the elusive Nirvana of a proper meditative state.

One afternoon the yogi had come across me crying in one of the gardens.

'Don't think!' he commanded, and he pressed his thumb into my forehead and rocked my fingers until they cracked.

'I'm trying!' I wailed, frustrated at wanting him to understand that while it was all very easy for him to say, he had absolutely no idea about my life or my feelings and so he couldn't possibly understand that he was asking the impossible of me. I had come to the conclusion that I couldn't do it, and that was that.

'I know you are trying.' He smiled kindly. 'But you are not doing.'

He bent down and picked up an exquisite frangipani bloom, freshly fallen from the fragrant tree. He looked at it closely without saying a word, lifted its sweet perfume to his nose for a moment, and then handed it to me.

'Look at this flower,' he said. 'See how beautiful it is.'

I looked at the flower in my hand, and as I admired its beauty in a moment of silence as he had, for the first time I caught a tiny glimpse of a peaceful mind. I had kept the flower until it wilted, looking at and thinking only about its beauty to the exclusion of all other thought.

'The healing process takes one hundred days,' Santash said patiently.

This evening, I had told him that I wanted to stop the treatment and spend the rest of my time here enjoying my holiday like a normal human being instead of putting myself through the misery of this personal mincer every day. We were sitting and talking in his room, and he had directed someone to bring us some herbal tea and asked if I had time to sit and talk for a while. It would have been churlish not to.

'For the first seven days, the body and mind reject treatment,' he explained. 'It believes that your disease is the normal state, having been used to it for all that time. It tries to retain the disease, and fights your attempts to remove it.'

I listened.

'After seven days, the body has no choice other than to surrender. At that point, we expect to see pain, catharsis and emotional outpouring come to the surface, as it can do at any time during the process. This is all quite normal.' He took a sip of his tea. 'The healing then continues in twenty-one-day cycles, taking one hundred days before reaching its full effectiveness.'

I took note of what he was saying and sat there feeling like a spoilt, ungrateful child.

'You will start to feel better tomorrow,' promised Santash. 'And when you go home, I will give you the medicines you need to finish the treatment yourself, and then you will feel completely fine.'

I went to the garden early the next morning before anyone else arrived for yoga, and took a seat on the grass beneath one of the spreading palms, checking first that there were no coconuts on that side of the tree waiting to drop onto my head and put an end to my suffering. There are a good few deaths each year caused by coconuts falling onto unsuspecting tourists, according to the guide book. But today I wasn't suffering. I felt clear-headed and calm. My day had begun as usual with the gentle knock at the door which came with the arrival of the herbal tea, and I had sat out on the verandah with it while I examined the clarity of the messages I had inexplicably woken with.

- I must empty my head, take and learn from its contents, and start again.
- This one life is a gift, and I had come this close to throwing mine away.

As I sat there under the palm tree, breathing deeply and expelling with each outward breath the futile feelings that had bound me by the wrists and ankles for most of my adult life, I let go of the pain and the guilt and decided that today would be the fresh start. Never again would I compromise myself or make myself unhappy just to please someone else.

I do not have to be what other people want me to be.

I am free to be who I want.

'Helen! Helen!' shouted the beach ladies when they saw me. They were strictly barred from the hotel's cordoned area, which was patrolled by a grumpy security guard who must have been impossibly uncomfortable standing out there all day in the sweltering heat.

I ventured out of the patrol zone and joined them in the shade of one of the long fishing boats pulled up onto the beach.

'Today, I have brought something for you,' I said, and I set down the big pile of things that I had heaved down to the beach from my room. In it was most of the baggage I had brought with me. Clothes, cosmetics, shoes, pointless accessories, all the toiletries and stationery from the hotel room, hairbrushes, a couple of beach bags, in fact everything that wasn't absolutely essential to my survival for the remaining day before my journey. I had been met with a few suspect glances from the guests as I puffed past the pool like a displaced bag lady, but I think they had written me off as mad (too much sun) and even Meg had stopped bothering me.

Trying to share everything out fairly was a bit tricky, and a few arguments broke out before I promised to return briefly the next day to give them the flip-flops and T-shirt I was still wearing.

With each piece I gave away, I felt a certain sense of relief, as though I was finally exorcizing every last part of the existence that had once been mine before I saw the light and my life was so generously returned to me.

I called the clinic from the telephone at the beach bar and cancelled my evening's appointment, explaining that in the two weeks that I had been there, I had not yet just sat quietly on the shore and watched the sun go down over the ocean. Santash was understanding, and said that he would send to my room the prescription that he had prepared for my imminent departure.

As the sun began to sink into the horizon, so began its breathtaking evening performance, streaking a magnificent blaze of orange and crimson across the sky, then changing dramatically to an impressionist's palette of purples and pinks as the day took itself off to shine its warmth upon the other side of the world.

'Beautiful, isn't it?' said a voice from beside me, and I looked up to see Godfrey taking a cigarette from his pocket before lighting it and settling himself onto the sand beside me and handing me one of the two Cokes he had brought with him.

He held up his bottle to me and we clinked them together and said cheers before returning to the achingly beautiful closing sequence from the natural panorama that stretched as far as the eye could see.

'It gets dark quickly,' he said softly. 'You must be careful walking alone on the beach in the dark. Sometimes it's not safe.'

'But I'm not alone.' I smiled, and we sat there and watched the local children try to fit in a last couple of runs before the light faded and they couldn't see the cricket ball any more.

'You are going home tomorrow?' he asked.

'Yes,' I answered sadly, and I looked at my feet as I pushed deep channels into the sand with my heels, thinking how nice it would be if I could stay just a little longer. I thought about home and wondered if I was ready to take on the responsibility of starting a new life.

'Would you like to stay with me tonight?'

Godfrey was gazing out towards the last gasping ribbons of colour shooting their way across the horizon, and for a moment I thought he was asking his question of the fading sky.

CHAPTER 11

FASTEN YOUR SEAT BELT

Considering what went on, it wasn't surprising that I didn't make it back to the beach ladies the next morning to hand over the shirt off my back. In fact, it was touch and go whether I was going to make it back to my room at all in time to throw my few remaining belongings into a bag and get to the airport for my flight home.

Now, as we taxied down the runway and I looked at the sand still stuck to my toes, I attempted to make sense of the last two weeks and tried in vain to tear my thoughts away from the award-winning pageant of the night before. I watched the cabin crew go through the motions of pointing out the emergency exits and pretending to pull oxygen masks over their faces, their expressions set with determined boredom and their eyes wandering around aimlessly as they ran through the safety procedures. Perhaps it's a deliberate technique designed not to panic nervous flyers, adopted as the furthest thing they can think of from the terrified expressions they would really adopt if faced with a legitimate mid-air disaster.

I gave them my undivided attention. After last night, I had too much to live for and there was no way I was going to risk not coming back alive on account of not knowing how to tie a double bow or find my attention whistle. The head-rushing tummy-drop sensation of the aeroplane taking off vertiginously into thin air at full power was as nothing compared to the lift-off I had experienced last night.

To be honest, I had never understood what all the fuss was about with sex. Overrated would be the understatement of the century, and I don't know a single woman who rushes home early at the prospect of having it off with her husband (unless she has an ulterior motive in mind, like a new handbag, saved up for that moment of post-coital weakness). And once the kids come along, you can pretty much forget it, mate.

Last night, I had had my eyes opened (among other unmentionable things) and now there was no going back.

In truth, the only slightly awkward part of the evening had been the first kiss. I didn't know whether to be demure or to go for it, so Godfrey had ended up kissing me while I thought about it and I forgot to react at all. If he found it strange it didn't show on his face, and by the time I had got the hang of it, he had already moved things along a little and I was too embarrassed to open my eyes. When I did, he was smiling at me, the soft light glowing against his skin, and mine looking like porcelain against his.

For the first time ever, my body revealed itself as a veritable theme park of wickedly pleasurable parts. Godfrey had quite apparently brought along a queue-jumping multi-pass for every ride in the book, and soon I began to take leave of my senses as he reduced me to a quivering mass with the internal combustion power of Mount St Helens on the verge of a monster eruption. Such was the intensity of the encounter that I had honestly thought at one point that I was going to die, and Julia's sound advice about not going on top once you're over thirty-something because it makes you look jowly went right out of my head.

The uncontrollable physical onslaught of my first orgasm was possibly one of the most frightening things that has ever happened to me in my life. I don't know how to say this as a grown (but obviously not very worldly) woman, but I honestly didn't know what it was. I genuinely thought that I was having a fatal seizure, my life about to be ended horribly in the most humiliating and ugly of circumstances, and by the time I realized what was actually going on, I think half the sub-continent must have heard my blood-curdling scream.

'Ssshhh,' whispered a worried-looking Godfrey holding his finger in front of his lips. 'This would look very bad if somebody were to call the police.'

I let go of his ears and apologized.

Then I asked him if he knew how to do that again.

Dragging my utterly spent self back to the hotel in the morning under the suspicious eye of the earlymorning malis tending the gardens, I thanked my lucky stars for the weeks of yoga and hoped that it would be enough to keep me out of the casualty department when I got home.

I had had to take the steps up to the plane one by one, sideways, for fear of snapping the hamstrings that had been so perilously wrapped around my sexual tour guide and the underside of a hammock for most of the preceding night.

'Yoga,' I explained to one of my fellow passengers as they watched my painful progress. They nodded their immediate understanding.

A few hours into the flight, I could feel everything seizing up with the unstoppable determination of a bent politician. Lifting the headphones onto my ears had triggered off an excruciating crescendo of pain in my triceps and shoulders. Upon reaching up into the overhead locker to retrieve one of the pashminas I had liberated from the outrageously-expensive-for-India hotel boutique, I had winced so loudly that the stewardess rushed to my assistance and got it down for me. She helped me cover my knees like a granny and tucked one of the little white airline pillows behind my aching neck. Sand dropped out from my hair, and she mentioned that I had quite a bit still left in my ears.

'Straight off the beach onto the plane?' she asked.

'Something like that,' I told her.

As if sensing my reluctance to go home and face up to my future, I decided to find something serious to worry about, and imagined myself being carted off to the emergency room with a deep-vein thrombosis brought on by my inability to move a muscle during an eleven-hour flight after screwing my brains out all night with a virtual stranger. My attempts at the ankle-rolling exercises started off an unbearable chain re-action of cramp then pins and needles so I hauled myself tenderly out of my seat and started a couple of laps of the aircraft in the hope of dispersing the blood clot that had almost cer-tainly now formed in the concrete muscles of my right leg. Check out page forty-seven of *The Illustrated Karma Sutra* and you'll get my general drift.

Making my way slowly through the scan-dalously cramped economy rows, I got the dis-tinct feeling that someone was staring at me. It's that personal radar deep inside that picks out the sensation of burning as a strange pair of eyes bore into you. It was on my second pass that I noticed the young man with the goatee beard and colourful beaded hair braids looking at me.

As I caught his eye, he looked pleased and smiled. Maybe he was some nutter off the beach who thought he knew me.

The strange thing was that his face was definitely very familiar, but I had absolutely no idea either who he was or why I should know him. Perhaps he's a minor celebrity. There are so many of them nowadays that it's only a matter of time before they outnumber us poor anonymous civilians two to one. I retreated through the mini-curtain to the D-list hangout of premium class and ate a couple of Nurofen.

'Hi there!' greeted the goatee as he fought his way towards me through the gathering crowd in the baggage reclaim hall. Do I know you? I'm sure the perplexed expression on my face must have given the game away.

'You don't recognize me, do you?' he said cheerfully. 'Probably these!' he added as he held up one of his plaits.

A waif-like hippy girl dressed in ethnic cotton prints with matching beaded hair appeared at his side. Great. The Brady Bunch. And they think they know me. He put his arm around her and introduced us.

'This is the woman I was telling you about who I saw on the plane,' he said to her.

'Oh right!' she said. 'Hello!'

'I'm sorry,' I started, 'but I'm afraid I really don't have the faintest—'

'Dorking College?' he interrupted. 'Modern car maintenance classes?'

I had buried the memory of those classes so deeply that for a moment I thought he must be mistaken. Then it slowly started creeping back. The long journey each week to the college so far away from my home. The way I hadn't told a soul what I was doing. The certain knowledge that I would never bump into anyone from there ever again.

My hand went to my mouth and I felt the blood drain from my face. It can't be. I looked again closely and saw that it was. Dave the petrol head. Only now he was Dave the petrol head with beads. I had shut both him and that entire chapter of my life firmly out of my mind for evermore, and now here it was, standing in front of me and shouting my past from the rooftops.

'She was my star pupil!' he proudly announced to the girlfriend. 'Came to all three of my courses even though one of them was a repeat!'

I felt sick down to my stomach.

'Remember?' he said to me happily. 'You were really interested in all the complicated stuff. Incredible! Most women can't even be bothered to find out how the handbrake works, never mind the on-board computer!'

Mercifully, one of the perks of flying premium class is that you get your baggage handled on priority. As the first red-tagged cases skidded down from the luggage chute onto the carousel, I spotted mine and lurched forwards to retrieve them.

'Let me do that!' said Dave, and he stepped out in front of me and pulled off the two bags I pointed out and then steadied them onto the luggage trolley for me.

'I have to go,' I stammered, and I fled towards the exit.

'Blimey,' said the girlfriend, 'she looks like she's seen a ghost.'

I felt the eyes of the customs officials burning into the back of my head as I passed through the green channel. If anyone looked like they had something to declare at that moment, it was surely me. I wondered if I should stop and hand over the contraband I had packed so undetectably in my heart, wrapping each layer with reams of silver duct tape to throw the sniffer dogs off the scent.

Nobody challenged me, and as I emerged through the official gateway to my home country, I threw off the ill-fitting cloak of remorse and left it to be trampled on the floor where it belonged.

CHAPTER 12

WAGON WHEEL?

As I stood by the space-age refrigerated display contemplating the life-extending merits of the bio yoghurts filled with germs, I threw caution to the wind and picked up the multi-pack of Gü chocolate puddings instead. They were so addictive that I was sure they had to be laced with crack, and at one point I was getting through so many that I considered cutting out the middle man and spreading it straight onto my hips. With those same hips now a good size smaller, I resolved to restrict myself to one pack a week. Oh all right then, two.

The doddering old lady standing next to me, bent almost double under the burdensome weight of her advancing years, and trying without too much success to read the side of a carton of cream as she leaned heavily on her trolley, caught me looking at her and shook her head sagely.

'I do wish they'd stop moving things about,' she clipped cheerfully in fluent Joyce Grenfell, her bemused gaze looking around at the bright, newly expanded supermarket. It had recently been transformed from an intimate neighbourhood store into a modern monster with bigger departments, deeper trolleys and a self-service cafe overlooking the unfinished car park. Still, that's progress for you.

'Used to be able to whip round Waitrose in ten minutes flat,' she said. 'Now I can't find a thing! I could be in here for hours!'

I nodded my agreement and moved along with a smile. I wondered if that would be me in another thirty-six years, shuffling my way through unintelligible ranks and files of products I neither recognized nor understood. No doubt it would all have moved on several quantum leaps by then and supermarket shelves would be a thing of the past, replaced by automated household appliances that refill themselves as if by magic while the mighty global Tesco helps itself to the stratospheric cost of our daily bread direct from our invisible electronic bank accounts.

I ran into the old lady again at the meat counter, where she had ground to a dazed halt under the relentless pressure of yet another overwhelming wave of product saturation.

'There's too much choice now,' she sighed upon seeing me. 'I don't know how you young people do it, I really don't. It's all just so confusing.' She looked nonplussed as she scanned the infinite rows of ham resting in expensive packets with slightly different titles. She shook her head.

'Yes,' I agreed with her. 'I remember the days when ham was just ham.'

My thoughts were transported to my eight-year-old self, my mother's shopping list written in longhand and tucked safely into my pocket with a big, old-fashioned five-pound note. I would walk down to the parade of shops at the bottom of our road, visiting the baker, the butcher, and the two old ladies who ran the grocery shop.

'I suppose it's because I lived through the war, you know,' said the old lady as she gave up on the ham. 'And we didn't have *anything*!' She emphasized the anything with a long gesture of her hand and nodded her head wisely as she remembered the way that they used to manage on virtually nothing plus the vegetables they could grow in the garden that was once filled with her grandmother's vulgar cat-wee chrys-anthemums.

'An ounce of this, a ration of that,' she said. 'That's if your father didn't go and swap it in the pub on the way home for a pouch of tobacco, of course! I console myself with the thought that at my ripe old age I won't have to put up with it for much longer.' She chuckled.

I laughed with her and we continued on our separate paths. I took my route through the quiet aisles at a leisurely pace, admiring the fresh fish laid out on the beds of crushed ice in the spanking new fishmonger section, stopping for a little chat with the man and admiring his giant turbot, resisting the cakes and pastries on the shelves of the French-style patisserie, trying out the nifty instant wine-cooling device that they've installed next to the beer display.

Now that it's just me rotting on my own at home with no sign of anyone to cater for but myself, I can't think of anything to buy, rather like getting to the supermarket and having a huge attack of amnesia. I pick things up, realize that they're only going to sit around and go off in the fridge, then put them back.

I used to do all my grocery shopping in a carefully planned routine of military precision in response to the daily battle of the endless meals I had to cook. Steaks on a Friday, roast on Sunday, tiresome dinner party on Tuesday, that kind of thing. With that particular whitewash now removed from my life, I hardly needed to be here at all. The days I had previously filled with the duties of chief cook and bottle-washer now lay strangely empty and stretched out before me like a blank canvas. I kept looking at it, but couldn't think of anything to paint.

The truth was that I liked it in here. I enjoyed looking at all the pristine products set out so beautifully in the well-lit, wide-aisled luxury of the shop I wasn't allowed to use before because it was too expensive. That wasn't to say that I didn't sneak in now and again to buy myself a few lunchtime delicacies which I would hide at the back of the fridge behind an unappetizing decoy cunningly fashioned from broccoli. I always made myself a nice lunch. Something small and tasty that I would often sit and enjoy in the company of the lunchtime heated debate on the television. Perhaps I should go back to the fishmonger's, pick up a couple of those enormous lobsters and wear them home.

My mobile rang just as I was pulling out of the car park. Leoni's name flashed up and I hit the handsfree button. I was getting rather good at that, having scared myself silly on the first couple of attempts when I'd looked back up at the road to find myself veering dangerously near to the kerb.

'Hey, Leoni!' I shouted.

'Hi there, stranger!' she said, her voice almost drowned out by the crashing and yelling in the background. 'I'm desperate to see you and to hear all about your holiday,' she gushed. 'But I've got the period from hell and I don't want to leave the house. It'll only end in disaster. Do you want to come over for coffee? I thought we could lie around on the carpet and eat all the kids' Wagon Wheels with our jeans undone.'

'On my way,' I said, and I turned right instead of left.

'You can keep your rotten old Wagon Wheels,' I said, putting the carrier bag down on Leoni's kitchen table. 'Get your laughing tackle around this,' and I pulled out two of the little chocolate puddings and handed one to her.

'Oooh!' she said, inspecting the hard plastic pot. 'I've not had one of these before.'

'Eat it and weep,' I said, and she pulled off the lid and buried the little spoon into the velvety goo, sinking into a vocabulary of 'Mmm' and 'My God, really mmmm' with her mouth full for the five minutes it took her to demolish it.

'Better?' I asked her.

'Much. My sugar levels have been beeping dangerously all day. So, tell me all about India,' she said as she put two big spoonfuls of fresh coffee into the pot and filled it from the kettle before reaching up for the mugs. She brought the milk and sugar to the kitchen table and left the coffee to mash.

'Did you bring any photographs?'

'No.'

'No?' demanded Leoni. 'No photographs? Are you mad? I don't want bloody anecdotes, Helen. I want hard evidence!' She banged her fist softly on the table and looked at me excitedly. 'I want to see beaches and tanned young men lying next to swimming pools in shockingly indecent thongs, and pictures of incredible shops selling all the stuff from Harvey Nichols' home furnishing department for fifty pence!'

'It wasn't that kind of holiday,' I said. 'I just didn't think about taking any pictures.'

'Yes? And? So?' she pressed on, squinting her eyes at me hard to indicate that she would detect instantly if I left anything out or tried to slip in a white lie.

Quick, switch to diversion tactics.

'But I did remember to bring this,' I announced, and I stood up gallantly and pulled out of the shopping bag the lovely pastel embroidered pashmina that I had picked out for her from the sinfully big pile I brought home with me. I had kept it in the car on the off-chance that we would see each other sooner than expected. She gasped and tore it from my hands, throwing it around her shoulders and rushing to look at its reflection in the mirror above the dining table next door.

'It's gorgeous! Gorgeous!' she enthused. 'And it's my colour! Oh thanks, Helen!' and she gave me a kiss.

'You're very welcome,' I said. 'And there's a whole lot more where that came from so don't expect any surprises for the next five birthdays.'

'Fine by me,' she said, picking up the edge of the shawl around her neck to study the fine needleworked flowers scattered across the corners.

'And?' she pushed me on the arm playfully. I smiled at her and refused to be drawn into her demand for some deeply juicy gossip.

'Oh come on, Helen. You must have done *something*? You must have met *someone*? Don't tell me you just hid in your room for two weeks doing nothing because I won't believe you. And don't tell me that that smile on your face doesn't have a certain ring of I've Had Sex about it either.'

Does it? I thought. I wanted to go and have a quick peek in her mirror to see if I looked any different. I certainly felt different, but I expected that to wear off after a while. Post-holiday elation, I had dubbed it, and to my shame I had found myself thinking some very inappropriate thoughts at surprisingly unsuitable moments. Like watching the young man who loaded my car for me at the supermarket, and the window cleaner's assistant who insists on taking his shirt off in the warmer weather and hanging it tantalizingly on the rose bush. Well the hydrangea had needed cutting back a little more that day anyway, otherwise I wouldn't have been in the garden to notice. Honestly.

'Really, Leoni,' I assured her, 'I didn't go anywhere and I didn't do anything wildly exciting. What I did do was an awful lot of serious thinking and I decided that I've got to take control of my life instead of pussy-footing around.'

'Good for you,' she said firmly, picking up her coffee mug and resting her elbows on the table as she cradled its comforting warmth in her hands.

'I've let a lot of years slip by without even realizing it,' I said quietly.

Suddenly, I didn't feel the need to hold on to the Hoover Dam any more. With hindsight, I think that one of the reasons I had kept all this to myself for so long was because I felt such an idiot for getting myself into such an intractable mess in the first place. I found the overflow valve and eased some of the strain on my bucket. I didn't care what people thought about it, or what they thought about me. If they didn't like it, they could all go and get stuffed. This was who I was. This was Helen. And if I couldn't start by speaking my mind and being honest with my best friend, I might as well call it a day really.

'You know, Leoni, I really thought that happiness was the domain of the young, that I had had my time, and that my life had naturally moved on to a different, normal phase where such feelings and demands had no place. That to want happiness as part of the long-term adult process was to hold the unreasonable expectations of a petulant child. Robert told me that this was what marriage was like.'

I looked at Leoni and shook my head.

'And I believed him. What I didn't realize was that this was what *my* marriage was like. It wasn't like that for everyone. It was like that for me. I feel so stupid.'

'I'm so sorry,' said Leoni.

'I asked him for a divorce once and he just laughed in my face.'

We sat there and sipped at our coffee in comfortable silence, each one of us running through in our heads what the perfect response would have been in such a nasty situation, rehearsing different actions and rapier remarks, each one more scathing than the previous, until the spectre of the husband withered and disappeared into the floor.

'How about, "Fuck off, you arsehole" then you pull out a big gun and shoot him in the grillocks,' said Leoni.

She reached into the shopping bag and took

out the two remaining puddings and handed one to me. We tore off the wrappers in silent unison. I picked up the teaspoon I had used to stir my coffee and licked it clean before digging it hard into the chocolate and pulling a generous spoonful off into my mouth. The unctuous paste temporarily locked my jaws together before melting away with a little assistance from the warm coffee.

'Mmm,' I said, 'that would have done the trick.'

I held the empty teaspoon in front of my face and looked at my elongated reflection in the back of it, then turned it around the other way so that I could see my head upside down. I moved the spoon around a bit, distorting my reflection to try to see what I would look like if I had a really slim face, but I couldn't get the proportions right and so I went from looking like a racehorse to resembling an alien with a Mekon head. Leoni pulled her trusty spoon from her chocolatey lips and pointed it at me.

'Or, "Well that's your decision, mate, but I'm pregnant with Mike Tyson's baby and he's just dying to meet you, you bastard."'

'Good one.' I laughed, and we did a high five.

We returned to our coffee and allowed ourselves to stew in the momentary euphoria of an inter-national chocolate hit for a little longer as we considered the outrageous lie that I had taken as read. More fool me. I had soldiered along with the full-size jungle pack, surviving on quarter rations, believing that this was the marvel of marriage and I was lucky to have it.

Had I murdered someone I would have served less time.

The last inch of coffee was just enough to release my mandibles from the final spoonful of the sickly rich pudding. I dropped the spoon into my empty coffee cup and stretched my shoulders back to release some of the tension I had unwittingly heaped upon them. Must do some yoga when I get home, I thought. My muscles had just about managed to knit themselves back together by now, so I really needed to take them out for a spin before I slumped into my old habits completely.

'Wagon Wheel?' asked Leoni, waving the open packet right in front of my face.

'I reckon so,' I said, and we retired to the sitting room to lie among the toys on the carpet in front of the television, undid our jeans and finished the whole packet.

Carol came to her door wearing a fetching floral-print housecoat. She was that kind of a woman. I could hear her singing in the kitchen as I reached the front door. She was belting out the ling-along-a-housewife favourite, 'Tie a Yellow Ribbon', with such gusto that I felt it more polite to wait until she had finished before ringing the doorbell. The doo-wapping bit at the end started to wear rather thin after a couple of choruses so I gave the bell a good old push to save her blushes. The burly chassis wailing stopped and she turned the radio down.

'Helen!' she said. 'Do come in!' She was drying up a saucepan and had brought both it and the tea towel to the door with her. She waved the pot around towards the kitchen and I followed her in.

'Nice holiday?' she said.

'Wonderful, thanks.'

'Where did you end up?'

'Spain.'

'Oh very nice,' she approved. 'Good weather?'

'Yes, lovely,' I said.

'How marvellous! Oh, you've got quite a lot of post. I'll get it for you.' And she went into one of the kitchen cupboards and pulled out a pile of letters, magazines and assorted junk.

'I know you probably won't want it all,' she explained, 'but I kept it all for you anyway, just in case.'

'Thank you, Carol. You're an absolute star.'

'Oh yes. And here's your key.'

She was obviously busy doing something so I didn't stay for coffee. Rather, she didn't invite me. As I let myself out of the door and stood on the step for a moment organizing the bundle of post in my hands, I heard the radio go up as Carol launched into a karaoke-kamikaze rendition of 'Karma Chameleon'. Go, Carol, go.

★   ★   ★

Sitting neatly back at my own kitchen table, I sorted through the correspondence and rejected ninety per cent of it as rubbish. That was a lot of people being paid to produce a lot of expensive garbage that's not read, wasn't it? Add together the cost of the people being paid to produce it, the cost of making it, bung on the price of a stamp, and that just didn't make sense, did it? Or was I being stupid or something? I know I'm not good with figures, but I reckoned that was more millions than I could count and it was a complete and utter waste of money, while we watch children starving in front of our eyes on the news. I could get very confused thinking about things like that.

Fortunately, though, I knew how to Not Think, as patiently taught to me by my very serene and now highly fashionable yogi. So, whenever an unwelcome or confusing thought came into my head, I could clear it almost immediately by concentrating my highly trained mind on a single point of focus, as demonstrated by the beautiful frangipani flower in the Garden of Eden.

Except that I found it far more effective to think about sex. Or more specifically, a certain type of hair-singeing Godfrey sex which cleared the mind of all other thought rather effectively. With this method, I could stay in a deep meditative trance for hours. Transcendental it might not be, but tantric it most certainly was. Try it. I think you'll find that a wholly satisfactory and genuinely hypnotic state is just moments away.

Ooh. What was this? It looked rather interesting. I examined the Air Force blue envelope with the confident handwritten address and set it to one side. Mmm. And another bill. I wouldn't open that yet. Put it to the other side. Oh now here was another interesting-looking one. Last in the pile, a deep embossed crest on the back of the envelope announced that this was not an ordinary letter. Indeed, it was a very important letter with a booming, gruff voice. So there. I acquiesced to its Royal command and slit open the envelope with the paring knife.

The letter from Julia's solicitor was polite and intriguing.

It went along the lines of, Dear Mrs Robbins, I am pleased to inform you that this firm has now concluded its enquiries in relation to your late husband's estate. In order that we may discuss our findings with you further, I would like to invite you to meet with me here at our offices, where I would be glad to explain everything to you in detail. Etcetera, etcetera, etcetera.

I read his suggested date and realized that it was the day after tomorrow. The letter was dated almost two weeks earlier, and I looked at my watch. Don't ask me why, I just did.

'Julia?'

She sounded like she was in a meeting.

'Can you talk?' I asked.

'Yes, but make it quick,' she responded before

220

saying to whoever, 'Bear with me, this is important. Won't take a minute.' There she was again. Dropping everything and making time for me. Anytime, anyplace, anywhere.

'I've had a letter from your lawyer and he wants me to go to a meeting with him on Thursday morning at ten o'clock but I only just got the letter and will you come with me?'

'Sure,' she said. 'I'll get Sara on to it. Call you later.'

'Bye,' I just managed to slot in before she hung up.

I felt a bit better and went back to the mystery letter from the confident hand. The inside of the envelope was lined with tissue paper in the same blue, and out of it I pulled a notecard scribed in the same style. It said, *Darling Helen, Will I ever have the pleasure of your company for dinner or are we destined never to meet again? Goodbye, cruel world. Dudley.* And he had added a kiss just before the postscript: *You can save me by ringing.* Then he left his number. As if I would have thrown it away. I held the card to my chest daintily and looked at my rather pleased reflection in the mirror.

Perhaps I might have his children after all.

That evening I did something that I had never done before in my life. I don't know what on earth possessed me to do it, but I took a long, hot shower, changed into something fabulous (that's fabulous for me, but not for someone like Ava Gardner), rang for a taxi, and took myself out to dinner. I know it's hardly the Ivy, but the local special-occasion-expensive restaurant isn't half bad, and on a Tuesday night I had no trouble at all getting a table. At first, the waiters had assumed that I was one half of an over-eager date, but I announced to them loudly enough not to be apologetic that I was dining alone and asked for their best table.

Thereafter they became utterly charming, all of them, and it was without doubt the most romantic, special dinner that I had ever had. And I didn't hide behind a book or a magazine either, although I had slipped into my hand-bag the letter I had received from Sheila that morning announcing that she had thrown Graham out on his ear on account of his being an insufferable shit, just in case I had wanted to amuse myself again with her stream of badly spelled vitriol.

I treated myself with the utmost deference and charm, taking my time over the gastronomic menu with a delightfully refreshing aperitif, selecting my very favourite things like the thinly sliced avocado with dressed crab and a little rocket salad, followed by a perfectly pert cushion of lamb which flushed pink under the embar-rassment of its own deliciousness. I asked the wine waiter to bring me a glass of whatever would go best with each dish, and smiled to myself as

I secretly watched the few couples who sat together being in love and clinking their glasses in endless toasts to their good fortune.

I basked in the warmth of their happiness, and felt entitled to sit and be among them.

CHAPTER 13

UNLUCKY FOR SOME

'Ah Mrs Robbins. Good of you to come.' The pinstripe-suited Mr Levine greeted us in his monstrously expensive office suite, saying, 'No calls, Sandra,' to the secretary who had collected us from the exquisitely furnished reception where we had waited patiently in air-conditioned comfort while he finished an important call to Germany.

'I am so sorry to have kept you waiting. It's a particularly nasty case involving some rather dubious characters who seem to have skipped the country,' he explained as he helped me remove my raincoat and hung it up on the old-fashioned mahogany hat stand. 'They've left the most enormous deposit with the firm and the bail was well into six figures so it makes you wonder, doesn't it?'

'And Julia,' he said, turning to her and taking her hand. 'I trust all is well with you?'

'Marvellous, thank you, Peter.' And she took a seat in the comfortable deep-buttoned green leather chair next to mine.

'Right. Well let's get straight down to business, shall we?' he said, landing heavily in his most distinguished captain's chair, unrolling the string on the buff document folder lying in readiness on his desk. He opened up the folder, then sat back and rested his fingertips together, looking at me intently over his half-moon spectacles.

'Mrs Robbins,' he began.

'Please, call me Helen,' I said.

'Yes of course, Helen. As you know, your husband died without leaving a will. That's what's known as dying intestate. It's all pretty straight-forward really. Lots of people don't think about making a will until much later in life or when they have children, and as his wife, you will naturally inherit everything anyway and you don't need to worry about things like inheritance tax and death duties.'

'That's a relief,' I said, looking at Julia for support.

She smiled at me reassuringly then returned her attention to the senior partner.

'You received the monies from the life insurance policies already, I take it?' he asked.

'Yes. Thank you.'

'Good.' He checked a few figures on the listed columns on the top document.

'By our calculations you should have received something of the order of three hundred and forty thousand pounds. Give or take,' he added without looking up.

'Yes,' I said. 'It was about that.'

Julia turned and stared at me, a faint smile

creeping across her lips, and she raised her eyebrows and crossed her legs before turning back to Peter.

'And then of course, there's the house,' he went on. 'The outstanding mortgage has been cleared by the endowment policy.' He looked up at us and cracked a financial services funny, 'Which is about the only thing they're good for these days!'

We both offered a little laugh.

'Yes.' He looked back at the documents. 'The title for that is all clear now and we're just waiting for a bit of paperwork to come through, then the house is yours to do with as you please. Did anyone offer you coffee?' he asked, pressing the buzzer on his desk intercom. 'Sandra? Could you bring in some coffee, please?'

'Yes, Mr Levine,' came the tinny reply.

He turned back to me and smiled in a slightly frightening way which he probably thought was his best put-you-at-ease friendly manner, as rehearsed each morning when he finished brushing his newly capped teeth.

'You will also benefit from your late husband's pension plan which had a widow's clause in it, meaning that it will pay out to you a regular monthly income for the rest of your life. It should be quite a tidy sum. About eighteen hundred a month, but that's taxable. Certainly it should be sufficient to keep you in hats and gloves quite comfortably.' Great. Another chauvinist.

He looked at Julia, and I saw her gesture towards

him to get on with it. She had insisted on paying the legal bill and I guessed that this was going to be costing a lot more than your average high-street bloodsucker.

Peter Levine cleared his throat and swung his captain's chair a little more in my direction.

'Helen,' he began again, 'are you aware that your husband was the sole beneficiary of the very substantial estate left behind by his mother some eighteen months ago?'

I furrowed my brow and looked at Julia. She shrugged her shoulders. What?

'No? What estate?' I asked.

I cast my mind back to the nice but hardly fantastic house that she had lived in. She always took herself off on long, extended holidays and had a lady come and 'do' for her, so she was obviously not on the breadline. No single-bar heaters for her in the winter. No, it was far more likely to be a three-month cruise around the picturesque slag heaps of the Canaries. I admit that I had thought it very odd that she should have signed the house over in some kind of equity-release plan that guaranteed her the right to live in her own home until she died, but meant that her estate forfeited the house upon her death. She just wasn't that kind of woman, and I couldn't imagine the Royal Marines being able to remove her from her house against her will, never mind the men in white coats. Besides, Robert had gone on at her ad infinitum about not doing anything stupid with his inheritance and I think he had even managed to get her to sign over power of attorney to him. Perhaps I was mistaken. It was all such a long time ago now.

The equity-release scheme was apparently run for the benefit of an age-related charity, and Robert had said that there was absolutely nothing that anybody could say to his mother that would make her change her mind, and that we really had no right to contest her will if that was what she had expressed as her final wish. I thought he had taken it very well actually, considering all the times that he had speculated on the money that she was worth, saying that one day it would all come to him, and that she had a lot more than anyone imagined. In fact, I really thought that he was going to blow a gasket and that I should make a reservation there and then at the nearest battered-wives shelter. But he just took the whole thing in his stride without so much as a murmur.

In the event, we didn't get a penny. She had died almost four years ago but the probate had dragged on and on and, according to Robert, by the time it had all been sorted out there was nothing left after the scandalously high legal and executor's fees. Robert had seemed remarkably unfazed by the whole disappointing outcome and had gone off to play golf for the weekend, no doubt to console himself away from the sympathetic noises I had been making to him for months. He didn't even bother telephoning home for the next couple of days, so I assumed that he was in pieces somewhere and needed to work it through on his own terms.

All his efforts and hard work, for nothing.

'Yes,' said Peter. 'It was a very complex affair by the looks of it, and because the funds were placed offshore, they took quite a bit of tracking down. I must say, Julia, that girl of yours – what's her name, Sara? – well, she's got quite an eye for detail, hasn't she? I'm not sure we would have made the discovery were it not for the odd little bits of paper she brought to my attention. Quite a gal, I'd say!'

He continued, 'Ah yes. Here we go. It's all perfectly in order and we have confirmed the amount. The death duties were all taken care of on declaration of probate so this is a net figure.'

He turned the piece of paper around the other way and leaned across the desk, placing it on the well-worn leather surface in front of me and taking his pen from his inside pocket. He removed the lid and pointed his inky nib towards the bottom of the column of figures, marking a little cross against the final total at the end of the page. I stretched forward from my chair and tried to look as though I knew what I was reading.

The door opened and in came Sandra with a tray. We all sat bolt upright and stopped collaborating while she poured the coffee and asked who wanted milk and sugar before handing the drinks around and leaving the room. We watched her close the door before returning to the confidential huddle. Now fully tooled-up with some serious caffeine, Peter brought my attention back to the piece of paper with a sharp tap of his pen. Ink spilled messily from the nib and he inspected the tip accusingly.

'If you look . . .' he turned his head sideways so that he could read it with me, 'just here.' He pointed.

I've never been particularly good with numbers, especially big ones, and I thought that I must be misinterpreting what I saw. Either that, or the figure had been presented to me in *lira*. Two point eight million. Let me just say that again for the benefit of anyone who didn't hear it the first time, like me, for example. Two, point, eight, MILLION.

'Two point eight million pounds, Mrs Robbins. Sorry, Helen.'

Oh yes, won't forget to use my first name now, will you, mister? I expect I'm going to come pretty high on the list of your new best friends.

Julia was staring at me with her eyes and mouth wide open.

'Shiiiiit!' she eventually managed. Then turning to Peter, 'Are you absolutely sure?'

'Oh there's no doubt about it, Julia,' he said calmly. 'We've gone through all the proper channels and while there's every reason to suspect he may have been deliberately trying to conceal the money from your sister . . .' He looked at me. 'I'm sorry, Helen, but he does seem to have gone to an awful lot of trouble to keep these funds well and truly locked away. If you ask me, all the evidence points to a man who had every intention of keeping his windfall to himself. Such as the postbox number he used for the account correspondence.' He addressed both of us again, 'But it was all properly declared for taxation purposes and I can assure you that the funds are as real as can be, and the entire amount is due to you, Helen.'

'What? Tax free?' Julia said.

'Tax free,' Peter confirmed, and he sat back in his chair and took an elegant sip of his coffee.

The room began to close in on me, and I just had time to hear Peter press his buzzer urgently and shout, 'Sandra! Bring a glass of water! Quickly!' before the lights went out.

'I don't believe it,' I said.

'Nor do I,' said Julia.

We were sitting in a cafe just off Wigmore Street trying to get over the shock of the news.

After recovering from my BAFTA-winning faint and emerging into the midday sun from Peter's office, we had looked at each other in stunned silence and sought the immediate refuge of a cappuccino with a large brandy on the side. The waiter must have thought we were a very strange pair, sitting there in a catatonic state and shaking our heads at each other in disbelief.

'You're a fucking millionaire,' Julia said

incredulously. 'Three times over. I thought I was going to be the millionaire, given another five years of hard labour, and now my little sister's not only beaten me to it, but raised the stakes a couple of squillion notches.'

'Yes. Sorry about that. It does seem a little unfair, doesn't it?' I felt a terrible fraud.

'Sod that!' she said. 'The way I see it, it's the compensation you properly deserve for putting up with Robert all these years. The sneaky bastard! What do you think he was going to do with all that money?'

Julia hadn't meant to say that last part out loud, and she apologized for being insensitive.

'No,' I reassured her, putting my hand over hers and leaning towards her. 'It's a bloody good question, actually.'

I had already answered that one in my head the moment Peter presented us with the evidence in his office. Far more troubling to me was the chilling question of how Robert had intended to get me out of the picture before running off with his fancy woman.

The brandy burned my throat as it followed the hot coffee, and I put the thought out of my mind. Who gave a toss about what Robert thought he was going to do with the money, anyway? It was mine now, and he could fuck right off. I hoped he could see me smiling from the furnace of his hell-hole while he shovelled rocks into the devil's fire for all eternity. Good riddance to bad rubbish.

And thanks for the cheque, sucker. I intended to spend every last penny of it on myself and on loose young men who know exactly how to amuse a merry widow like me. So up yours, Robert. May you rot in hell.

I threw back the last of the cognac and set the glass down on the table.

'Shall I get the bill for you?' Julia asked, finishing her coffee and reaching for her bag.

I was miles away and looked up at her for a repeat of the question. She misinterpreted my stare.

'Well I'm not bloody well paying!' she said.

CHAPTER 14

NEW BEGINNINGS

Two glorious days. That's how long it took to mobilize my grand Coming Out dinner. I was suffering from acute cold-turkey haute-cuisine withdrawal symptoms and needed the rush of a class-A cookery fix, so I decided to put my yen to good use and resolved to cook as I had never cooked before.

After poring diligently over a library load of recipe books for hours and calling dozens of specialist suppliers to source the rare-breed and verge-of-extinction ingredients I had decided upon, I began composing a masterful production of perfectly pitched flavours. No expense would be spared and no stone left unturned in my obsessive pursuit of culinary perfection. The fluttering exhilaration I felt as I opened and decanted the mail-ordered delicacies essential to the Michelin-starred final outcome spread the unseasonal spirit of Christmas in the late summer of my restless home.

The time passed in a blur of peeling, chopping, blanching, soaking, mixing, reducing, resting, baking and chilling. It was not without its hazards.

In a momentary lapse of concentration I accidentally grated my new, longer-length fingernails in with the lemon zest, rendering the first batch of dressing unusable and my manicure a write-off. And after faffing around for ages with the langoustines and lacerating both my thumbs on their spiteful little pincers, I decided that they were more trouble than they were worth so gave the whole lot to the ginger pigeon-slayer from number forty-four.

It was while I was feeding Fatso and telling him about my plans that I realized the pheasant was on the critical list. Its ten-minute rapid sear in a warp ten oven had somehow extended into a half-hour suicide mission. After burning up on re-entry, there was no resuscitating the patient. It was well and truly DOA. I pulled the smoking pan out of the oven and left it to finish incinerating itself outside.

It didn't really matter. The haunch of venison was big enough to feed an army anyway, and I had more shellfish than I knew what to do with. I had got rather carried away when I placed the order, and wondered if I should not have put 'elasticated' next to the dress code on the invitations.

Tenderly, I bruised the leaves of the fresh herbs I had picked in the dewy mist of first light from the pots on the patio, and laid the final touches to the banquet now ready to cook. The kitchen table groaned under the bountiful piles of trimmed vegetables and baking trays. Every inch of surface was covered, and everything I needed to orchestrate my concerto was now ready and within my reach. I turned on the radio, fired up the burners, and set my flashing pans upon the flames.

With everything finally done, it was time to go upstairs and pull out the old brown cardboard box which had been shoved to the back of the ward-robe in the spare room under a dust sheet for as long as we had been there. It was much heavier than I anticipated and took some deter-mination to move. I carefully carried the box back to the kitchen and slit the almost perished brown packing tape with a sharp knife. Opening the tattered flaps I gently removed the rustling layer of shredded newspaper from the top and lifted out the first piece from the exquisite wedding service I had never used.

It had been left to me as a gift by my wonder-fully intuitive and eccentric grandmother, to be given to me on the occasion of my marriage. I remembered that the first time I had seen it, it had taken my breath away. So delicate and beauti-ful was it that I had never dared to use so much as a side plate, and I had squirrelled it away again with the romantic notion that I would one day pass it on to a daughter of my own.

I felt bad that it had been so sadly neglected, locked away and forgotten for thirteen years, poised patiently for the day that never came, and as I washed each piece and dried it before putting it in its rightful place on the dining table, I resolved to enjoy the legacy of its momentous charms every day.

Placing the finishing touches to the heavily laden table, I believed that I had truly excelled myself. I returned to make a quick progress report on the imminent triumph limbering up in the wings, then went upstairs to put on my red dress.

The guests finished their drinks and settled themselves into their preferred seats after playing a protracted game of silent musical chairs and changing their minds several times until they found the perfect pecking order. The conversation quietened with anticipation.

I presented the opening masterpiece to a hushed audience, took my place at the head of the table, and raised my fork to the others.

'Eat,' I said, and the table fell silent under the bewitching spell of the taste sensations that exploded in unison around the smiling faces.

'My God!' exclaimed Marcus. 'That's the most delicious thing I've ever eaten! You're a bloody domestic goddess!'

Switch the domestic for sex and you might be somewhere in the right ballpark, honey, I thought to myself secretly.

'You really do know the way to a man's heart,' he declared, filling his mouth again without a hint of inhibition and soaking a hunk of bread into the hot, spicy butter.

'Too right,' added Sara. 'This is totally orgasmic. Isn't shellfish an aphrodisiac?'

'I bloody well hope not,' said Leoni as she concentrated on her plate, 'or he's sleeping in the garage.'

'You know, darling,' Marcus addressed his wife enthusiastically with the blunt edge of his knife, 'I think you should make these next time we have a dinner party at home. You'll hand over the secret, won't you, Helen?'

'I've got a better idea,' said Leoni cuttingly, heading him off at the pass. 'Next time we have a dinner party at home, why don't you bloody well cook it yourself, then it'll be just buggering perfect, won't it?'

Marcus smiled and tried to protect himself as Leoni lunged at him with an asparagus tip, pretending to stab him in the neck while flogging him with her napkin. He quickly regrouped his position and retaliated, fighting back hard with a piece of bread, and biting the end clean off her weapon. Leoni waved her shattered spear in his face then quickly popped it into her mouth and pressed her thumb on his nose hard enough to make him say ouch.

'You should open a restaurant,' declared David, looking at the delicious morsel impaled on the end of his fork. 'I'd definitely come. This is just incredible.'

He washed away the ecstatic taste with a velvety mouthful of the soft, peachy Viognier that the gentleman at the wine merchant's had assured me was the perfect foil to the succulent clams which had been flown in that very morning courtesy of the manager at the lovely restaurant where I had enjoyed my extravagant dinner-for-one. I explained my menu to the merchant in great detail, and he had dispatched to me a case of wines, each one with an old-fashioned handwritten swing-tag dangling around its neck, dictating when and how it was to be served. He had even noted the correct temperatures, with timed opening instructions for each precious bottle.

'Tastes like perfume,' observed Sara, staring into the swirling vortex she had created in her glass as she practised her best television-wine-expert technique. She stuck her nose deep into the glass and sniffed so hard that some of the wine shot up her nostrils causing her to choke and splutter horribly, and she waved her arms around in demonstration of her urgent need for an extra napkin.

'The trouble is, Helen,' started Julia earnestly, 'you go around cooking stuff like this, and the next thing you know, we're all expected to be able to rustle up a Gordon Ramsay special without so much as smudging our lip gloss.'

'Abso-bloody-lutely,' agreed Leoni. 'We would be perfectly within our rights to brand you a traitor.'

'No pudding for you,' I told her sternly.

She gave me her best hang-dog expression and stuck out her bottom lip just like Millie does.

David pulled softly on Julia's sleeve, leaned into her ear and whispered something confidential. She looked at him intimately and laughed.

'Oh don't you two start,' said Sara with her mouth full. 'Get a room.'

By the time we got to dessert, the table was rocking with laughter and easy conversation. The candle-light played across the cheerful faces and spread their warmth all around me.

My pièce de résistance of dark Valhrona choco-late parfait with kirsch-soaked cherries received a rowdy crescendo of whistling, applause and table banging as it arrived to a loud school-dining-hall cheer. David got up to open another bottle of wine.

'Hey, David,' called Julia.

David turned around to see her lob a fat ripe cherry high into the air above his head. He took one step to the right and caught it perfectly in his mouth without breaking rhythm as he uncorked the wine.

Leoni was already into the main event.

'Oh my Gog,' she mumbled through the pudding, pointing back at it with her spoon. 'This is sodding unbelievable.' Her eyes glazed over.

'So what's next, Helen? Now that you're rich as Croesus and free as a bird, we're all dying to know what your plans are,' asked Marcus as he drained his glass and waved it at David for a top-up.

It was the question burning on everyone's lips, but only Marcus was pissed enough to have forgotten that they had all bloodied their thumbs in a pre-dinner pact to keep schtum. A hush fell over the table.

'Marcus!' snapped Leoni, giving him one of her finest Darth Vader death stares.

'What?' he said. 'It's only what we're all sitting here thinking, isn't it? God, I haven't heard you talk about anything else all week, woman!'

Leoni shot an embarrassed look of apology to me as Marcus ploughed on, seemingly oblivious that he had just put his wine glass down smack in the middle of the puddle of raspberry coulis on his plate.

'She doesn't mind! Do you, Helen? I mean, Christ,' he opened his hands in papal address to the table, 'we're all friends here, aren't we?'

'Please, Marcus, don't apologize.' I smiled at him. 'In fact, that's the reason I asked you all here tonight.' They all looked towards me and waited expectantly. I stood up.

'I would like to propose a toast,' I said, lifting my glass towards my friends. 'To new beginnings.'

The carnage in the kitchen the next morning kept me busy for a good couple of hours or so. It looked like a scene from *The Texas Chainsaw Massacre*. I had thought it better to leave the dishes as they were last night rather than try to wash them up with fingers generously buttered with several large glasses of Burgundy or whatever it was. Surveying the wreckage now, it occurred to me that it might be a lot easier just to torch the place and claim on the insurance.

To my great sense of satisfaction and pride, there was not a single scrap of anything left from the dinner. I found the button from Marcus's trousers on the carpet while hoovering behind the television. We all heard it go ping but it had ricocheted off the wall and no one saw where it went. As I put away the last of my grandmother's plates in the cupboard, the little blue coffee pot on the hob gave out a heated sigh and I set it to one side while I warmed the jug of milk in the microwave.

With the kitchen finally spotless, I took the shopping-list pad from the drawer next to the sink and found a pen in the old earthenware mustard pot on the dresser. I settled myself at the table with my coffee and turned my thoughts to the list I was about to write. The Grand Plan. The pad looked up at me expectantly. I tapped the pen against my lips and returned its winsome gaze.

The doorbell rang. Oh for heaven's sake, what was it this time? I put the pen down crossly and went to answer the door. I should have looked through the window first.

'Helen!' enthused Graham. His hair was shower damp, and his trousers freshly pressed. He had brought something with him wrapped in a carrier bag and tucked in the crook of his arm. It looked suspiciously like a bottle of champagne. I glanced up at him wearily and said what I should have said weeks ago.

'Oh, do piss off, Graham.' And I closed the door firmly on his stunned expression. A few moments passed and the doorbell rang again. I ignored it and went back to the kitchen, turning up the radio and closing the door behind me. It was agony hour, and I wanted to be sitting comfortably.

I returned to my list. This time, I had no hesitation.

- Sell the house.
- Change telephone number.
- Take my old name back?
- Find someone debauched to have sex with.

My mind went blank.

I got up and mooched around the kitchen, aimlessly poking with my finger at the miniature gravel surrounding the cactus on the window sill and looking out to the garden at nothing in particular, then poured myself another coffee. Sitting back at the table, I picked up the pen and resumed my thoughts.

As I daydreamed a technicolour vision of the unsung life that lay ahead of me, filled with promise and a new-found courage, a distant voice drifted in from the radio. It was soft and unbearably moving, finally breaking down and unable to speak. The kitchen fell silent under the shock of her statement before the presenter filled the empty airwaves with a few tender words of encouragement to her devastated caller.

'So, Susan,' said Anna softly. 'Tell me your story . . .'